SNOW BRIDES

A StormWatch Novel

PEGGY WEBB

WESTMORELAND HOUSE

Westmoreland House, Mooreville, Mississippi

First Edition January 2020
Print Edition ISBN: 9781706129806

Printed in the United States of America

DEDICATION

In loving memory of Jefferson

My gentle giant hundred pound chocolate Lab Jefferson was my faithful companion, fierce protector and biggest fan for fifteen years. Though he was not a Search and Rescue dog, he was the most loyal and steadfast canine friend a writer could ever have. We had a routine. Breakfast al fresco if the weather permitted followed by a brisk walk either in my spacious yard or on my farm. Then it was back to the office where he took up vigil under my six-foot table-top desk. Sometimes he'd rest his head on my feet while I wrote and sometimes I'd rest my feet on his warm body, particularly in winter. He took every break with me, entertained my guests, never begged for treats but knew they were his just due, and went with me to Florida to romp on the beach with my family there. He even submitted gracefully to being boarded while I flew to New Hampshire to visit my family in Concord. And when night came, he took up vigil on his doggie pillow beside my bed. He was splendid, and I still miss him. I felt his spirit as I named the SAR dog in this book after him and wrote of my fictional dog's intelligence, loyalty and great capacity for love. This one's for you, big guy.

CONTENTS

GRAND MARSAIS 9 NEWS

As Stanley Weathers faced the Channel 9 cameras he adjusted his tie and chafed at the latest ribbing he'd taken about his name. It had come from the new hire, some underling in the bowels of the TV station who obviously thought Stan had never heard anybody say, "A weatherman named Weathers? Did you make that up?"

When he got home he'd tell his wife Jean about it, and she'd find a way to make him laugh. *If* he got home. The snowstorm coming their way was a monster beyond anything he'd ever witnessed. He was going to have a hard time maintaining a cool professionalism during the weather report.

"Stan," the cameraman said. "You're on in two."

He put on his stage smile and faced the cameras.

"Holly is her name, and she's unlike any snowstorm we've ever seen." He gestured to the weather map behind him, tracking the storm as he talked. "The blizzard that has held the Northwest in its grip since December 12 is sweeping toward Minnesota. This killer storm has left a path of destruction across Montana, Colorado, Nebraska and South Dakota."

The death toll rose in his mind, and he paused, hoping his TV audience would perceive it as a planned break from his dramatic spiel. Stan was relieved the number of fatalities would be part of the news report, not the weather.

"Expect the blizzard to be one of the worst in the history of Minnesota with snow drifts as high as thirty feet. The mega-monster storm is on a path to hit Grand Marsais at 2:00 p.m. on December 23 and could last up to three days."

There went the big family Christmas. That was the only good thing Stan could say about the storm. Jean had already called to say her parents had sent a text from Atlanta that their flight had been cancelled. He would have enjoyed seeing them, but he couldn't say the same thing about Jean's obnoxious, know-it-all twin sister Joan and her two teenaged brats who were traveling with them.

"Residents are urged to cancel holiday travel plans," he told his TV audience. "Our team here at TV 9 News in Grand Marsais is standing by to bring you a list of airport closings. As always, Stan the Weatherman will be here at the station bringing you regular updates on Holly. Until then, stay off the roads. Be smart. Be safe."

CHAPTER ONE

DECEMBER 23
4:00 a.m.

"I SHOULD HAVE PICKED HER UP."

Joe left his vigil at the window that showed nothing except the distant shape of Carter's Trading Post and the ghostly outlines of security lights that seemed to float above the water in the snow mists swirling through the darkness. A heavy blanket of snow had fallen on Grand Marsais during the night and the temperature had already dropped below zero, both precursors of the blizzard predicted to hit in early afternoon.

Maggie's big chocolate Labrador retriever lifted his head at her husband's uncharacteristic display of nerves then left his pillow by the fire and padded to lean against Joe's leg.

It was uncanny, Jefferson's ability to sense the emotional terrain of his family. Though Maggie shouldn't have been surprised. The four-year-old search and rescue dog had displayed extraordinary intelligence from the moment

1

Maggie started working with him. Even better, he had more heart than any dog she'd ever handled.

He was feeling their pain.

Their daughter Kate was missing, and had been since yesterday afternoon.

"You should have let me go after her," Joe added as he sank onto the sofa, his face etched with worry and defeat.

The worry, Maggie shared, but if she let herself dwell on Joe's sense of defeat and the many reasons why, she wouldn't have the strength to get through this long vigil for her daughter.

"Don't start, Joe."

Hadn't Maggie told herself the same thing a thousand times during the last sixteen hours? Kate, a freshman at the University of Minnesota in Duluth, reveled in her newfound freedom and had scoffed at the idea she couldn't drive a hundred miles north for the holidays.

"Mom!" Even on the phone Kate's most exasperated, long-suffering daughter tone had been evident. "I'll be home long before this so-called monster storm hits."

"You be careful. And start early. Don't wait till the last minute."

"I'm loading the car now. You worry too much, Mom."

That had been nine o'clock yesterday morning. During normal winter conditions snowplows kept the roads between Grand Marsais and Duluth clean. That far in advance of the storm, Kate should have been home before noon, even in holiday traffic.

To make the nightmare even worse, her GPS tracker showed she'd veered far off course. Maggie had been flabber-gasted when her daughter's GPS put her in Chicago. And the last time she'd checked, Kate was in Detroit and moving northeast.

A thousand horrors played through Maggie's mind--her

daughter skidding off the road and landing in a spot hidden from highway traffic then picked up by a predator who could do anything. Haul Kate out of the country or easily vanish into nearly four million acres of wilderness known as the Superior National Forest. The idea of her daughter in the hands of a predator struck terror to Maggie's soul.

"Don't go there." The sound of her own voice calmed her a bit, but her mind still spun in all directions.

What if Kate had arranged to meet someone, a guy her parents didn't know, someone she'd met online? It happened all the time, vulnerable young girls with bleeding hearts falling for a sob story only to be lured off then led like lambs to the slaughter.

That didn't sound like something her levelheaded daughter would do, but who knew how she might have changed under the peer pressure on a college campus?

"Joe, I'm going to make a cup of coffee. You want one?"

"No. I'm good."

He wasn't good. Any fool could tell by looking. She wasn't good. *They* weren't good--and hadn't been for a very long time.

She was glad to escape to the kitchen. She popped a pod into the coffeemaker then made the call she didn't want Joe to hear.

Ten years ago he'd have been right with her, taking turns as they called on their network of friends in law enforcement who knew them as two of the most successful search and rescue handlers in the U.S. Now everything about SAR, with the exception of Maggie's dog, sent Joe scrambling backward into a private world of his own making, one with walls so thick and so high Maggie had no hope of getting through.

Longtime friend, Detective Roger Dillard, picked up on the first ring.

"This is Maggie Carter. Any news?"

"Kate has stopped moving. Her GPS tracker shows her in Toronto."

The shock felt as if somebody had drained off all Maggie's oxygen. Coffee forgotten, she sank into a chair.

"That's impossible! She doesn't know anyone there, and she'd *never* go off like that without telling us."

"Are you sure about that? Maybe she had a secret boyfriend and is planning an elopement. It happens all the time."

"Not with Kate. You know how responsible she is." Roger's daughter Teresa had been one of Kate's best friends since kindergarten. The Johnson's house was her second home. "Something awful has happened. I just know it."

"I've already contacted the authorities in Toronto, Maggie. As soon as they locate her cell phone, I'll let you know."

"You're going to continue your search, aren't you?"

"Of course, I am. I love that kid like she's my own." The line went quiet and Maggie thought she'd dropped the call. Then Roger cleared his throat. "We've already covered a lot of territory north of the college in Duluth, but with the storm closing in, I don't know how long I can keep my men out here."

"You owe me, Roger." This year alone, Maggie had found four missing children for him and dozens of other missing persons through the years, both with her chocolate Lab and the air scent dogs who had come before him.

"I promise we're going to do everything we can to bring Kate home."

"Thanks. I know you will."

Maggie wasn't about to believe her daughter was in Canada.

She was torn between screaming, crying or racing into the night with Jefferson to start her own search. But where to

4

start? Though air scent dogs, unlike tracking dogs, didn't need a last known location for their search, they did need a general area as a starting point. Without one Maggie and her dog would waste precious time randomly plunging into a search in the hundred-mile stretch between college and home. Time she couldn't afford to lose with a blizzard heading their way.

Law enforcement had questioned all the people who saw Kate last—her roommate, the guard at the campus gate, the owner of the service station just off campus where she always refilled her gas tank before starting home. Kate, the good girl, heeding her dad's advice: Always drive from the top of your tank. You never know what will happen. Driving from the bottom is too risky.

They all remembered her, cheerful, calling out happy holiday greetings and waving as she started toward home. The service station was the last place anyone had seen her, but the manager recalled seeing her drive away and head north.

Maggie grabbed her mobile phone and tapped on her daughter's name in Favorites. How many times did that make since yesterday morning? Ten? Fifteen?

Hi, this is Kate. Leave a message.

"Kate, where are you? If you get this, please, please call me. Even if you've done something you think we won't approve. Your dad and I are worried sick."

Maggie could barely function. The Christmas china she'd dragged out for her daughter's homecoming lunch still sat on holiday placemats, forlorn and hopeless looking among the remnants of a meal they never ate—home baked bread getting hard on the platter, the creamed corn Kate loved, Joe's favorite apple dumplings, his mom's recipe for broccoli salad with cranberries and nuts. The only thing Maggie had rescued from the uneaten meal was her oven roasted turkey. Perfectly cooked, waiting for the meal that was supposed to bring them all back together again, now sitting in its own congealed fat in the refrigerator.

She broke off a piece of bread and nibbled around the edges. Yesterday morning when her life had still been halfway normal, Joe had come into the kitchen while it was baking.

"Something smells good in here."

"Yeast-rising bread. Apple dumplings, too." She pointed to the casserole dish cooling on the sideboard."

"You've gone all out. Kate bringing somebody home?"

"No. It'll be just the three of us. I want this holiday to be special, Joe. Like it once was."

For a moment he looked gut punched. Then he'd smiled in a pale imitation of the way it used to be. "I think I'd like that."

The one word, *think,* had said more about the state of their marriage than all those nights she'd reached for Joe only to find his side of the bed empty and him sleeping on the sofa with Jefferson on the wool rug beside him.

It had spurred Maggie to take desperate measures. She'd tried to seduce her husband in the kitchen. She didn't care where they landed, the floor, the table, propped against the kitchen sink with the faucets poking into her hips. She'd just wanted proof the spark was still there, no matter how small. She wanted to believe their marriage wasn't dead; it was only in hibernation until some great spring-thaw moment would make it bloom again.

Her spring-thaw moment was a disaster. She'd been clumsy, he'd been awkward, and both of them had been relieved when Maggie's cell phone rang, bringing their pathetic attempt to a halt. He rearranged his clothes while she scrambled for her phone. By the time she found it, she'd missed a call from daughter.

Mom, something's come up. Don't know when I'll get home.

Ten little words. They meant everything and nothing at all.

Kate hadn't answered when Maggie called back. Her daughter's message was the last anybody had heard from her since yesterday morning. And yet, they offered no details. So far search choppers had reported no accidents on the interstate to block traffic, no detours. Why had she called to say she'd be late? Where was she?

Maggie could no longer bear to sit still. She started clearing the table, stowing the clean dishes back into the cupboard, dumping the wilted salad, tossing the corn. The apple dumplings would still be okay. She put them into the refrigerator then grabbed the bread to toss. On second thought, she sliced off the hardened edges then wrapped the soft center in foil.

Joe appeared in the doorway and just stood there saying nothing, his expression speaking volumes. *Everything is gone and I don't know how to get it back.*

Maggie whirled toward him, hands on her hips. "What?"

"Nothing."

"You always say that, Joe. We never talk anymore. Not really."

"What do you want me to say?"

"How about, has Kate told you anything that might give us a clue what's going on?"

"Has she, Maggie?"

Suddenly her legs would no longer support her. She sank into a chair and rested her head on the table.

"Yes," she whispered.

"Yes?" Joe sat down at the table but he didn't reach for her hand, didn't offer her comfort of any kind. "Did you say *yes?*"

An unexpected fury overtook her and she jerked upright to glare at him. "Do you think our daughter's blind? Did you think she wouldn't notice you can hardly bear to be in the same room with me? That every time I head out the door on a SAR mission you hide deeper behind those walls you've built around yourself?"

"I don't even know how to respond to that."

"You can't stand to be home anymore, Joe. You spend more time on the Superior Trail leading guided tours than here."

"What are you getting at?"

"I don't know, I don't *know*." Maggie buried her face in her hands, groaning. If she let herself, she could fall asleep from sheer exhaustion. She forced herself back to life, made herself look at her husband. "Roger says the GPS tracker shows Kate's in Canada."

"That can't be right."

"I told him the same thing. But I keep wondering if she decided at the last minute to spend the holidays with a new college friend."

"She wouldn't do that without telling us."

"Maybe she did." Maggie pulled her cell phone from her pocket to replay her daughter's message. They both strained toward the phone as if they might reach inside and pull Kate to safety. "Maybe the *something* that came up was dread of coming home to parents who don't even seem to like each other anymore, let alone love. Just last week she asked me what was wrong between us."

"Nothing's wrong. And certainly nothing I'd want to discuss with my daughter." Joe shoved out of his chair and stalked off.

For what? To stare out the window? To bundle up and open the trading post?

Nowadays, trouble sent Joe racing toward the comfort of a familiar routine. But she couldn't begrudge him the escape. After all, here she was tidying up the kitchen at four a.m.

The phone she'd left on the table jangled and Roger's

number popped up. She seized it as if it were the last life raft on the Titanic.

"Hello."

"Maggie, we've found her car."

"Thank God! Just a minute. I want to get Joe." Maggie raced to the door and yelled for her husband, who came on the run. She punched speakerphone. "Go ahead, Roger."

"Kate's car is in the ditch on a small side road called Glen's Crossing about sixty-five miles south of Grand Marsais."

The ghost of a memory nagged at Maggie, and she felt the chill of an awful premonition. What was it? She was so tired she couldn't think straight.

"How is she, Roger? Is she okay?"

"She's not here. We found her suitcase in the backseat and a winter parka in the front."

"Kate would never leave the car without a coat," Joe said. "She's a seasoned hiker."

"What about her backpack?" Maggie tried to rein in her fear. More and more it appeared her daughter had been taken.

"We haven't found anything else yet. I've got deputies fanned into the woods searching but the snow last night covered any tracks we might have discovered."

"I'm telling you, Kate wouldn't have left the car," Joe said. "I know that area. It's isolated. There's not a single place nearby where she could have walked in this snow for help, particularly when she could have called us."

"Looks like she had a blowout and the front end of her car is smashed up pretty bad. Considering her GPS tracking information we can't discount kidnapping. I'm still waiting for a call from authorities in Canada."

Dread washed over Maggie, and a premonition so horrible she could almost see her daughter, rendered powerless by evil.

"Something about this whole scenario doesn't feel right, Roger. Give Joe the exact location of the car. I'll be there as soon as I can."

As Maggie raced out of the kitchen she heard Roger firing off directions followed by the caution, "Storm's coming. We don't have much time."

Didn't he think she knew that? The latest weather report from Stan the weatherman said the massive storm would hit northern Minnesota in ten hours.

Maggie raced into her daughter's bedroom and grabbed the raggedy old Pooh Bear off the bed. Kate had slept with it every night since she was born. The wonder is that she hadn't carried it to college with her. It would hold more of her scent than anything else in the room.

Air scent dogs, unlike tracking dogs, didn't need an article that belonged to the missing. They worked by sniffing the air for the trail everybody leaves behind, unaware--unseen skin cells and hair that float away when you pass through a place, even the gases you exhale when you breathe. Their uncanny olfactory ability was why air scent dogs were so valuable working landslides, avalanches and other freaks of nature and man that buried multiple victims under tons of debris.

Still, the scent-specific object would let Jefferson know beyond a shadow of a doubt he wasn't looking for multiple people. His job was to find Kate.

Kate's bear almost brought Maggie to tears. She hugged the stuffed animal, trying to comfort herself by touching something belonging to her daughter. Finally she said, "Get moving."

It was the sort of advice she'd once given Kate. When you think you can't go one step more, give yourself a pep talk. Out loud.

As she hurried about packing everything she'd need for a SAR search in the dead of winter, possibly in the middle of a blizzard, the memory she'd sought earlier hit her with a force that buckled her knees.

The snow. The location, not twenty miles from Glen's Crossing. The missing girls. Two of them, one year apart. Both college age, both blond. Like Kate.

Maggie had found both of them dead.

CHAPTER TWO

4: 45 a.m

"MAGGIE?" When she didn't answer, Joe found his wife sitting in the middle of their bedroom floor clutching Kate's beat-up old teddy bear. He knelt beside her. "Are you okay? What happened?"

"Nothing. Help me up. I don't have a minute to lose."

"You mean *we*. I'm going with you."

"You don't have to. You can stay here in case she shows up. Roger can be my base camp and Jefferson won't let me get lost."

"She's my daughter, too, Maggie."

"Fine," she said.

That was it? Fine? It felt cold, impersonal, and nothing like the relationship they'd once had.

He didn't point out that he knew the Superior wilderness as well or better than any air scent dog his wife had ever handled. He'd hiked the entire three hundred twenty-six miles of Superior Trail many times.

She'd been right about the amount of time he spent there. Nature was the world's greatest tranquilizer. The grandeur that was both beautiful and dangerous overwhelmed the senses to the point there was no room for anything except awe.

Joe hurried to load his four-wheel drive extended cab truck, shutting down his memories from force of habit. Jefferson jumped into the backseat and promptly curled onto his blanket. He'd be asleep within minutes. Smart dog, conserving his energy for the brutal search ahead.

Maggie climbed into the passenger side. "You got directions?"

"Yes."

Twenty years ago, when they met, she wouldn't have asked. They'd been paired together with their dogs, working a mudslide that had trapped hikers on the Superior Trail, and they'd trusted each other—and their feelings--as instinctively as they'd trusted their SAR dogs. Within two weeks he'd moved into her cottage in Grand Marsais.

"To see if our dogs are as compatible as we are," Joe had teased her.

"If they're not, I'm getting a different dog."

Theirs had been a perfect match, both human and canine. Joe had planned to work the search and rescue missions with his wife until they grew too old, and then spend their retirement fishing and boating and dropping hints to Kate to make them doting grandparents.

Now, Maggie sighed and leaned her head against the back of the seat.

"You should sleep while you have the chance."

"I can't." She turned to him in the darkened cab. "I'm fine."

Joe let her lie slide. The last time she'd said she was fine and really meant it, she'd been holding their baby daughter, watching him load up Clint, his German shepherd air scent dog, for the massive search and rescue after the 9-11 attack on the World Trade Towers.

He tried to shut down the memories, but the stress of his missing daughter and the lull of driving through the darkness in a silent cab on a road with few travelers opened a floodgate. The horrors he'd locked out for years came pouring back. The ash, everything covered with ash, the acrid scent of burning jet fuel, the charred bodies they'd found, one after the other.

There were so many dead, so many failures, that dogs accustomed to the excitement of finding the lost still alive became depressed. Clint's sense of defeat showed in his tucked tail, the hangdog expression when he stood back from the latest remains he'd found.

Finally Joe had come up with the idea of letting a few of the handlers hide and then sending the search dogs out so they could rescue someone alive. Canine morale improved so dogs and handlers could keep pushing forward, working against time and brutal conditions.

Joe had been getting ready to take Clint out for some rest when the big German shepherd gave the alert signal indicating he'd caught a scent.

"Good boy. Search." Joe patted his head and watched him trot once more into the rubble. That was the last time he ever saw his dog.

Just as Clint disappeared into the building there was an ominous rumble, the dreadful warning of collapse. Clint, along with dozens of other SAR dogs, died at the World Trade Towers, canine heroes as surely as all the first responders who gave up their lives for others.

The spirit went out of Joe. Guilt seared his soul. Clint didn't get to choose whether he wanted to be a search dog. Joe had chosen for him. He'd made the decision to send his dog into the horror of two collapsing skyscrapers in the aftermath of the unthinkable, a terrorist attack on American soil.

He couldn't bear the thought of sending another dog into harm's way, the agony of finding so many victims after a disaster of that scope. Joe always entered a search filled with empathy for the lost and the loved ones they'd left behind. Every tragedy punched a hole in his heart. He knew if he kept going with his heart wide open, he was heading for a breakdown.

And so he'd closed himself off from his feelings, built walls to keep the tattered pieces of his heart intact, remained silent hoping the nightmares would eventually subside.

Against Maggie's advice, he gave up SAR and built Carter's Trading Post, boat rentals and wilderness outfitters. If hikers also wanted a guided tour of the Superior Trail, Joe Carter was the man. He could control the hikes, set the rules, keep everybody safe.

What a joke. He'd managed to keep everybody safe except the ones who mattered most--his family.

Any fool could see how he and Maggie had drifted apart. They went their separate ways so often they hardly saw each other. Even when they were both home, it seemed they'd become polite strangers.

And then in September, after his heart-wrenching trip to Ground Zero for a ceremony honoring the dog heroes of 9-11, the gap between them had turned into a chasm. He'd lost his dog, his wife, his hope of a large family and the profession he'd once loved. Soon he'd lose his only child, who had entered her freshman year in college and in the blink of an eye would be packing to strike out on her own.

Life seemed pointless.

And now this. His daughter, gone. Maybe forever.

They were heading straight to the area where Maggie had

found those dead girls. Both posed in the snow. Joe couldn't bear to think about what might have happened to Kate.

He glanced across the cab at his wife. She was sleeping, finally. A small blessing. His wife couldn't see how the wind was picking up speed, how the previous night's snowfall was being lifted into the air, making visibility harder.

How long before there would be a complete whiteout? They hadn't even begun the search and time was already running out for them.

His stomach heaving, Joe eased onto the shoulder and lost what little food he'd had since he realized his daughter wasn't coming home.

CHAPTER THREE

5:00 a.m.

Run! Run! Run!

Fear and adrenaline pumped through Kate. She wanted to race across the long stretch of yard toward the trail, a mere gap in the trees barely visible in the woods up ahead. But *she* was watching, standing under a dim light in the doorway of the farmhouse, training her flashlight beam on Kate and smiling as if she were a favorite aunt sending her off for cookies and milk next door instead of toward a rough trail in snowy woods into the wild unknown.

Clutching the borrowed coat that was too big and far too lightweight to offer any protection from the looming blizzard, Kate made herself wave at Betty. She even made herself mouth *thank you,* though whether the woman would see through the snow swirling in the wind, she didn't know. Then she forced herself to walk away from the house of horrors as if she didn't have a single suspicion.

Keep up the charade. Act dumb. Play the helpless, scared female.

Kate was the exact opposite of the role she played. She had her mother's fierce spirit plus a shelf full of trophies from her days as the star of her high school cross-country track team as well as her cross-country ski team. She also had knowledge of the wilderness accumulated through years of tagging along behind her daddy on the hiking trails. She knew the location of every treacherous ravine and frozen lake on the trails she'd run, skied and hiked. Though a fat lot of good any of that would do in millions of acres of wilderness without skis, winter gear, or even the bare minimum supplies to keep her alive.

She had one granola bar Betty had tucked into her coat pocket.

"In case you get hungry before you get to the trading post," she'd said, then winked, as if the two of them had become best friends overnight and now shared some delicious secret.

The only thing Kate had in common with Betty was being trapped overnight in the same house with a raving madman. Still, Betty had been kind to her, and was the only reason Kate was now free. She vowed that if she ever got out of this alive, she'd make sure the unfortunate woman was rescued.

Kate kept a steady pace until she reached the protection of the trees and was out of the path of Betty's flashlight. Then she turned for one last look. Thank goodness Betty was no longer watching from the doorway. The entire house was dark. She hoped the poor woman had gone back to bed and, come morning, she'd find a way to keep Jonathan from following. Betty had promised to try.

"And that's all a mother can do," she'd said. "Put her whole heart into her child and then try to keep him on the straight and narrow. Jonathan is a bit irrepressible, but deep down he's a good boy."

Irrepressible didn't begin to describe that maniac.

Fear and the urge to run still clawed at Kate. If she took off running now, she could be at the store in fifteen minutes, even in the snow. Betty had given her explicit instructions. *Follow the trail...one mile to Wayne's Trading Post...right on the trail...telephone service...food...safe shelter from the approaching snowstorm.*

But what if Betty had given her the wrong directions or Kate had misunderstood? In the excitement of being tugged awake in the dark and hearing Betty's whisper, "Shh. I'm going to help you," Kate could easily have gotten confused. She wasn't a morning person. And if she got lost she certainly was not equipped to survive a long journey home through a monster snow storm.

Her belongings were in her car, but she had only a vague idea of the location in relation to Betty's house and no idea how far it was. Besides, her vehicle was the first place Jonathan would look--the same place where he'd found her.

Was it only yesterday?

It seemed forever since she'd headed home for the holidays. It seemed to Kate another girl had seen the detour sign, that someone not as savvy as she had turned her car onto the ill-kept road without a second thought then called home to announce her delay--right before the blowout catapulted her car over the edge of a small ravine.

The details surrounding her wreck were fuzzy—the brutal force of the airbag, her rescuer, big and rawboned, driving a snowmobile, asking if she was okay. The last thing she remembered was drinking hot coffee from his thermos.

She'd awakened with a horrible headache in an unfamiliar bed—and still struggled with a persistent dull throbbing.

As she paced herself toward the trail, memories crowded in...

The view from the strange bedroom window had shown a

snow-covered forest. What rural view in a Minnesota winter didn't?

Kate struggled to sit up, but her head was pounding so hard she flopped back onto the pillows and glanced around the strange room. It was sparsely furnished and very clean. But where was her backpack? Her coat? Her phone?

"Hello?" she called. "Hello? Is anybody there?"

The door opened and a tall big-boned woman with gray streaks through her blond hair entered carrying a tray filled with food.

"You're awake!"

"Where am I?"

"At my house, honey, and don't you worry about a thing. I've brought good hot beef and vegetable soup, my specialty." The woman set the tray on the bedside table then sank onto the mattress. It sagged under her weight. Up close her face still told the story that she'd once been a beautiful woman. "By the way, my son Jonathan's the one found you. I sent him back to your car to get your belongings."

"Do you have a phone I can use?"

"Phone lines are down and we have to go into Glen's Crossing to get cell phone service." The woman patted her hand. "I'm Betty, hon. What's your name?"

"Kate. Kate Carter."

"It's lovely to have another female in the house. Somebody to talk to besides my son. I bet you're a college girl."

"I am." Kate glanced at her watch. Already two o'clock? "Listen, I hate to be rude but my parents are going to be worried sick. I was supposed to be home two hours ago."

"Don't fret. As soon as Jonathan gets back with your things, he'll take the snowmobile into Glen's Crossing and call your parents. You just rest now. You had a nasty bump on that pretty head of yours."

When Betty left, Kate dug into the food, astonished at how hungry she was. The soup was especially delicious.

A loud click stopped Kate's spoon in mid-air. It was the unmistakable sound of a key turning in the door lock.

"No, no, no, no, no!" As Kate raced toward the door, pain exploded through her head. She caught the side of a dressing table and stood there a moment, swaying.

"What are you doing?" The voice beyond the door was male, loud and angry. Could it be Jonathan, the son?

"Cleaning up the mess you made." That was definitely Betty.

Kate rushed to the door and tugged.

"Betty? The door's locked!" No response. Kate started banging. "Is that Jonathan? Did he bring my things?" Still, nothing. "Betty! Open up!"

Why weren't they answering? Kate pressed her ear to the door, but all she could hear was the echo of receding footsteps.

"Wait! Where are you going? Come back."

Nothing. Not a single reply, not even another footfall.

Holding the side of her head, Kate explored the room, looking for any clues that would tell her more about Betty and her son. It was spacious but sparsely furnished, a double brass bed, a dressing table with a tarnished silver-handled comb, brush and mirror set. The bedside table held a copy of the King James edition of the Bible plus an outdated Farmer's Almanac. Had the furnishings once belonged to a great-grandmother? Or did Betty simply have a fondness for browsing antique shops?

Two rocking chairs with crewel-work cushions faced each other in the window nook. Kate's own grandmother liked to crochet, knit, and do embroidery and crewel work. Had Betty made the cushions? The question might start a conversation that would let the woman know she didn't have to lock Kate in. She was from a good, normal family. She wasn't about to go prowling around Betty's house stealing things.

Kate's head was pounding now. She nabbed a sandwich off the tray and sank into one of the rocking chairs.

And that's when she saw it. The snow scene was not outside the window at all. It was an enlarged photograph of a snow scene taped over the window. And behind it were iron bars.

Kate was a prisoner.

CHAPTER FOUR

Now, standing in the safety of the woods, looking back at the dark house, Kate shivered and pulled the thin borrowed coat closer. That Betty had helped her escape was a miracle. That she might not survive was a strong possibility. It was far colder than when she'd left campus, clearly below freezing and maybe even sub-zero. Frigid air bit through the inadequate coat as the wind whipped around her.

She needed more protection, and she needed it fast. The shed, barely visible in Betty's backyard, was Kate's best bet. People kept all kinds of stuff in sheds.

Keeping to the deep shadows, she sneaked back into the yard. She hoped Betty had gone back to bed. And she for sure didn't want to wake that monster son of hers.

Kate wasn't planning to steal. Just do some stealthy borrowing. If she found something she could use, she'd made sure Betty got it back. Along with a thank you note.

If she got home. *When* she got home.

It seemed impossible that only yesterday Kate's only serious thought had been whether Mom would insist she wear that hideous Christmas sweater Grandma Carter had knitted for her last year. Gran would be sure to notice. And though she had poor taste in clothes, she was a sweetheart. Kate couldn't bear the idea of hurting her feelings.

She wondered if she'd ever see Gran again. If she'd ever see any of them.

"Buck up." Kate said this aloud. It was a trick Mom had taught her.

She always said, "When things aren't working out the way you think they should, Katie, give yourself a little pep talk. Out loud. Sometimes all it takes to make you believe in yourself is the sound of your own voice."

Filled with a renewed self-confidence, Kate crept toward the door of the shed.

It was padlocked, but she found a window on the far side facing the woods. Without a second thought, she shucked her coat and wrapped it around a big rock to muffle the sound of breaking glass. Then she cleared away the jagged edges and hefted herself inside.

Hurry, hurry, hurry.

It was still dark outside, but goose bumps rose at the possibility of the creepy Jonathan catching her. When her eyes adjusted to the dark, she grabbed a penlight off a workbench and trained it around the walls.

Jackpot.

Three pairs of snowshoes. An ice ax and rope. A garbage bag filled with cast-offs, including winter gear. Feeling as if she'd just aced every one of her final exams, Kate selected snowshoes first. One pair was made for running, light weight titanium frames, fewer crampon teeth and bindings, and a narrow-waisted frame for better balance and maneuverability. She grabbed them and then dug into the garbage bag.

The ski suit she pulled out was pink—probably Betty's— far too big but thankfully long enough to fit tightly around the ankles of her boots. She nabbed a handful of extra socks from the bag, mismatched woolens--it didn't' matter—and an extra sweater with a few moth holes. She cinched the suit by wrapping the stolen rope around her waist then pulled on a pair of mismatched gloves and a full-face ski cap she'd found. She dropped the rest of her supplies out the window.

Training the beam of her light around, she searched for anything else she could use. A flash of red caught her eye.

Please, please, please.

Her heart pounding, she knelt to shove cardboard boxes aside. And there was her backpack, tucked into the corner beside an ornate carved wooden box.

Her hands shook as she unbuckled it and scrambled through the contents. Her wallet was there plus her thermos of water, a pack of beef jerky and her space blanket folded into a small square.

"No matter how short your journey, in the winter in Minnesota always prepare for emergencies," her dad always said.

If he were there, Kate would kiss him.

But where was her laptop? Her cell phone? She searched all the pockets of the backpack for her phone but came up empty. Had she taken it out when she called her mom? Left it on the front seat?

She thought not. Her phone was programmed with the hands-free system in her car. She *never* took it out when she was driving.

That cretin, Jonathan, had taken it. It had to be him. Kate unzipped her wallet and trained the small flashlight inside. Her cash was there and her credit cards. But, wait. Where was her driver's license? Why in the world would the jerk want her license?

She shivered. The possibilities were limitless, and all of them horrible.

"Just go," she whispered. "Take the backpack and go!"

But the carved box more than stirred her curiosity; it seemed to be exerting some strange pull on her. Ornate and even a bit feminine, it was totally out of place in a backyard shed.

Kate opened the lid. Inside was one gold earring in the shape of a unicorn and a charm bracelet with one bangle, a turquoise and silver dream catcher. She'd seen the bracelet before. Or one like it. Had it been in one of those gift shops that sprouted up like mushrooms in Minnesota's tourist spots?

As Kate dug beneath the jewelry, her flashlight glinted off something shiny. Plastic, maybe. She trained her light closer. It was a driver's license for Jennifer Olsen, blond, blue eyes, 5'3", Duluth, Minnesota. She was nineteen years old.

A chill ran through Kate. She remembered the bracelet now. Jennifer Olsen had been wearing it in the Missing Girl posters she'd seen in gas stations all over Minnesota.

The second license was for Linda Stephenson, blond, blue eyes, 5' 6", Fargo, North Dakota. Twenty years old. She'd gone missing a year after Jen.

Behind that was a third. Kate Carter, blond, blue eyes, 5'9", Grand Marsais. She'd turned nineteen in November.

Terror seized her. Jen's and Linda's bodies had been found in the snow, located by the SAR team of Maggie Carter and Jefferson.

There was something else, too, something so unspeakable Kate felt the bile rise to her throat.

When she'd searched her prison/room she'd discovered two doors. The first one led into a windowless bathroom with a small prefabricated shower, a toilet and a wall-hung sink with two toothbrushes in a holder on the porcelain lip. Two bathrobes hung on hooks behind the door, one pink, practically new and a larger blue one, well-worn.

The other door had led to a closet. Inside was only one

garment, a wedding dress with tags still on it. Size six. Kate's size.

Both Jen's and Linda's bodies has been posed in the snow with a single arrow through the heart and a wedding veil on their heads. Whoever murdered them had a sick notion that they were brides.

And Kate was supposed to be next.

"Not while I have breath."

She grabbed her driver's license, slammed the box shut then bolted through the window with her backpack. Outside, she gathered up her stolen gear and sprinted toward the woods.

Without breaking her stride she found the trail then ran as if the hounds of Hell were after her. That's what being around Jonathan had felt like, facing a whole pack of raving mad dogs bent on devouring her.

Pace yourself. Run smart. Coach Keith Lucas's voice brought her to a halt.

It played through her head as clearly as if she were back on the high school track training with her teammates.

Speed is not everything, Coach said. When Keith Lucas gave one of his famous pep talks, he paced along the side of the track, fists slightly balled, shoulders relaxed and arms loose and swinging as if he were running a marathon. *You've got to be mentally tough. A fearless mind is your biggest ally.*

Kate centered herself with some deep breaths.

"First things first," she said. The sound of her own voice was reassuring in the silence of the woods.

She strapped on the running snowshoes then mentally ran down the list of things she needed to do in order to run smart and strong.

If she didn't properly strap the ice ax to her backpack she was liable to have a mishap and cut herself so deeply she wouldn't have to worry about Jonathan. She'd bleed out before he ever found her.

Next she trained her stolen flashlight into the woods, checking out her surroundings, searching for her captor, peering through the gloom, listening for a single sound that didn't belong in the deep wilderness.

Except for the stirring of air from hawks on the wing and a flash of fur from a fox on the run, the woods were strangely silent. This close to Wayne's Trading Post signs of human life should be evident, tracks in the snow from other snowshoes and snowmobiles, a distant hum from air stirred by motors and human voices, radios turned too loud and the electronic dinging of the gas pumps, doors opening and shutting, the whine of traffic on a nearby highway.

Kate tamped down her rising panic.

Focus, Coach said.

In the darkness, the trail was discernable only because the gap in the trees allowed more light.

"I've got this," Kate said, and she felt the confidence pouring through her. She was a superb athlete, and her mom and dad would surely come looking for her. Were they searching already?

She broke the branch of a sapling beside the trail just enough to leave it hanging. For good measure she jerked off her ski cap and ran her gloved hands roughly through her hair, imagining her hair and skin flaking off in such quantity Jefferson would alert to the strong scent trail.

"There now." She got back on the trail and readied herself for a race that meant life or death.

Stay steady. Coach Keith Lucas cheered her on. *Finish strong.*

Kate relaxed her shoulders, slightly balled her fists and took off running, focusing on what lay ahead. Running in snowshoes was entirely different from running in track shoes.

She had to widen her stance to accommodate the shoes and lift her knees higher.

"I'm tough. I've got this."

Visibility was not good, but she could make out a sharp curve just ahead.

Don't follow the curves, Kate. Coach's advice played like a record in her head. *It increases the distance. Run the tangents.*

She stayed in the center of the trail, taking the straight line through the curve and the next two that followed.

Soon she was in a rhythm, running with ease, imagining her destination as the finish line.

But where was Wayne's Trading Post? She paused to listen for sounds of human habitation and got nothing except deep woods silence. Logic told her that this close to the holidays and with a blizzard coming, folks wouldn't be gadding about the general store. They'd be securing doors and windows, laying in a supply of wood for their fireplaces, checking their backup generators to make sure they had enough fuel to get through the power outages, checking their food supplies.

Still, she had to be close to the finish line.

"Forward, Kate Carter."

She picked up speed, racing against time. A storm was bearing down on her, and so, possibly, was a mad man.

CHAPTER FIVE

5:45 a.m.

SCREECHING tires and slammed-on brakes jerked Maggie out of a deep sleep. She lurched forward, her seatbelt sawing into her ribs as the truck skidded toward a ditch.

"Joe?" She braced her feet against the floorboard. "What the heck?"

"Don't know." He fought with the wheel, brought the truck out of a spin and came to a halt just inches short of a red Jeep Grand Cherokee stopped in front of him on the highway. A ghostly line of traffic was barely visible in front of the Jeep, their taillights glowing in the early morning darkness.

Gusts of snow swirled in a wind that was much stronger than when they'd left the house. The weatherman was right. The blizzard was coming, and it was coming on strong.

"Oh, no," she said. "How far are we from Glen's Crossing?"

"At least another fifteen miles."

And traffic wasn't moving. Most of the cars idled, keeping the heater on, but a few of the drivers had bailed out and were walking toward the front of the line.

"Wait here, Maggie. I'll see what I can find out."

"Sure." Maggie wanted to tear her hair out. All she'd done since yesterday was wait. And with each passing minute, her chances of finding Kate alive diminished.

Jefferson whined and stuck his nose over the back of her seat. He not only in tune with the weather but with her every mood. As she patted his head, she tried to tamp down her growing anxiety. "It's okay, boy. We'll find her."

With her dog in the car, the windows fogged quickly. Maggie wiped the moisture off with some paper napkins she found wadded on the front seat. When she shifted, two empty paper cups rattled at her feet. She spotted another on the back seat beside Jefferson. Joe had never been especially neat, but lately he didn't seem to care about anything, particularly picking up after himself.

She used to find his slightly messy ways endearing. Now, when she found a dirty towel on the bathroom floor or picked up a coffee cup he'd left on the table by his recliner, she was likely to say, "I'm not your housekeeper." And say it in a very snarky voice.

No wonder he couldn't stand to be around her.

"And vice versa."

When Jefferson whined again she realized she was talking to herself. Was she trying to convince herself of something? What? That their long history together made the marriage worth saving, or that it just proved they'd been doomed from the beginning?

What a ridiculous line of thought. Her only excuse was that it kept her mind off Kate and this horrible, unexpected delay.

"Maggie." Joe tapped on her window and she powered it down. "There's a four-car pileup ahead. It'll be hours before it's cleared."

"Oh, no."

"A little boy's missing from one of the wrecked vehicles."

"How could he be missing?"

"Both parents are so drunk they don't know how he got out or when. They've both been passed out and are still addled. They figure the kid bailed out after the wreck. Cops are already there. I told them you'd help."

"Of course."

As Maggie sprang into action, she prayed her daughter was out there alive somewhere, staying strong. *Hang on, Katie. I'm coming for you.*

Knowing what the harness and vest meant, Jefferson went into full search and rescue mode, posture erect, ears alert, his sleek body powered by muscles toned with exercise and proper diet.

"Good boy." Maggie leaned down to pat his head and then headed down the line of cars toward the wreckage.

The scene at the front of the line broke Maggie's heart, a man with a bloody bandage on his head, sobbing, the woman beside him wrapped in a blanket and looking shell-shocked as she and her husband took turns telling that that their little boy was only five. His name was Timmy. They had no idea why he left the car or where he was.

Skid marks showed where their blue Toyota had started sliding on the road. It had crossed lanes to hit an elderly man in an oncoming pickup truck. The two cars following had crashed into him.

The strong odor of alcohol wafted through the open doors of the Toyota.

Joe approached a young highway patrolman. Ken

Hawkins, according to his badge. "This is my wife, Maggie Carter, and Jefferson, the SAR dog I told you about."

"I'm grateful for your help, Mrs. Carter. We've got men searching the stretch of highway, but so far, nothing."

"I'll need something that belongs to the missing child," Maggie said. With all these people milling around, there would be scent trails everywhere.

When Ken approached the parents, the mother stumbled upright then sank into a heap on the icy road. It was the father who limped to the car and came back with a little red jacket.

"Is the child out there without his coat?" Maggie asked. If anything was more horrible than a lost child, it was one lost in winter without proper clothing. When the mother shrugged, Maggie wanted to shake some sense into her. How could she be so careless with a small child?

How could *she* be so careless with Kate? Why had she caved into the wishes of a stubborn teenager who didn't have the experience to make wise decisions involving traveling in snowstorms? Why had she brushed aside Joe's worries with that drivel about letting Kate test her wings, letting her grow up and be independent?

"Maggie?" Joe took the little wool jacket from the father and pressed it into her hand. "You okay?"

"I'm good. I've got this."

She led Jefferson away from the crowd to improve his focus... and hers. Squatting beside him, she let him sniff the jacket and prepped him for the search. Then she took him off lead and he set off in a trot in the opposite direction of the other searchers.

Within minutes her dog plunged down the embankment from the highway and loped across a field of scrub brush and stunted trees, cross sweeping for scent. In the distance Maggie could see the vague outline of a creek snaking through the field. She trained her flashlight on Jefferson and saw him streaking in the direction of the water.

"Oh, please, no. Please. Please."

She feared the worst. A scared little boy, a slippery bank, an ice-covered creek, some it of thick enough to walk on, some thin enough to crack apart and let a child slip through. If he'd gone into icy water, there's no way he would still be alive.

Would her daughter meet that same fate?

"Tim," she called, her voice cracking with cold and anxiety. "Tim!"

Jefferson was still going, his tail up like a flag, his nose pointed straight to the creek. Fear increased Maggie's speed. She prayed as she ran.

Suddenly, that abrupt halt, that bark—Jefferson's find signal. Even better, he was jumping up and down, his signal for *found alive*.

There was no doubt in her mind. No hesitation. If Jefferson had found the boy dead, he would be sitting.

"We've got him," she yelled. "We've found him. He's alive!"

On the road above, Joe shouted, "She's got him!"

Maggie heard the answering calls of other men, coming closer as they scrambled down the embankment and raced her way.

"Tim," they shouted, their voices echoing across the frozen field, held aloft and magnified by frigid air.

Jefferson had stopped just short of the creek. Maggie hurried the last hundred yards toward a large hollow log. She heaped extravagant praise on her dog then squatted down for a look. The little boy was hunkered inside, his lips blue, his eyes wide and his gray sweatshirt bloody.

"It's okay, Tim. You're safe. You can come out now."

Blinking against the glare of her flashlight, he shook his head—*no*—and refused to budge.

Maggie passed his red jacket to him. "You daddy wants you to have this, honey. He's waiting for you back on the road."

Timmy grabbed the coat and clutched it to his chest, but he still refused to move.

"Are you hurt, honey?"

That slight little shake of his head. *Yes.*

"Give me your hand and I'll help you out." She reached for the child but he scooted deeper into the log.

Suddenly Joe was beside her, squatted down with his face close to the log's opening.

"Hey, there, buddy. Your daddy Charlie sent me to get you. If you'll scoot up here, we'll go find him and I'll let you pet the dog."

"Okay."

And that's how simple it was, how simple it had always been for her husband to charm people, young and old alike. He scooped the little boy up then turned to smile at Maggie.

It was so like the look he used to give her after they'd found a missing person during their SAR days together that, for a moment, Maggie felt the years melt away. In the space of seconds, she found her heart warming toward her husband while an icy wind lifted her hair and sent a chill down her collar.

"Come on, Maggie, let's get Timmy back to his mama and daddy." Joe ruffled the little boy's hair. "Your Aunt Patricia will be up there waiting for you, too, buddy."

For the first time since his rescue, the little boy smiled.

When they got back to the accident scene, Timmy went straight to his Aunt Patricia while Joe consulted Ken about the quickest way to get them to Glen's Crossing.

"It's going to be another hour or so before we can clear a

path for you through here." Ken waved his hand toward the wreckage and all the emergency vehicles. "Your best bet is to go back about five miles and cut through the forest on Everson Road. It'll be slower driving but still, it will beat waiting here."

Ken wished them luck and they headed back to the truck. Jefferson bedded down as soon he loaded into the backseat. Maggie stripped off her gloves and held her hands in front of the heat vents.

"What will happen to that poor little boy, Joe?"

"Several people in the search party know the couple. They said both parents are repeat offenders. Child protective services will step in this time, and he'll probably be put in the custody of his Aunt Patricia."

"She seemed like a nice sort."

"There are still good people in this world."

"Do you think Kate found somebody like that?"

"I don't know, Maggie."

"The Glen's Crossing area is where I found those girls in the snow."

"I know. Don't think about it."

"It's sparsely populated. And remote." Joe didn't answer, and she couldn't bear to look at him and see her own anxiety mirrored in his face. "Could she have walked to a shelter somewhere?"

"Anything's possible."

"I don't want platitudes, Joe. You know that area better than I do. Is there someplace father away from where her car was found that most people wouldn't even attempt to go, someplace she could have remembered from hiking with you?"

"A couple of remote houses, but we never hiked that area together. She rode with me to Glen's Crossing on a business trip, but she was only eight."

"She's smart, Joe. Maybe she went to one of those houses and just can't call us for whatever reason."

"Without her coat?"

Maggie was grasping at straws. Desperate. Frightened. No, terrified. She didn't even ask how remote the houses were. She was scared of the answer.

"Hurry, Joe.'"

CHAPTER SIX

6:55 a.m.

KATE'S SPIRITS lifted as the pale slivers of light announced the approach of dawn. Running would be much easier now that she could see the trail.

A sudden gust of wind lifted snow off the forest floor. The powdery curtain obscured visibility and reminded her that a storm was coming. She stopped to rest and to get her bearings.

Where was the store? Kate had traveled as fast as she dared in her running snowshoes, trying to pace herself without getting overheated. At the speed she'd been going, she should have found the trading post long before now.

Had she passed the store in the dark? Betty had said it was right on the trail. Even under current conditions, Kate would have seen a clearing big enough for a store and a parking lot. She'd have seen the shape of a large building.

Obviously Kate had misunderstood. Or maybe Betty's directions were not accurate. She was probably under so

41

much stress from living with her unhinged son she couldn't think straight.

"Poor Betty. When I get out of this mess, I'll see that you get some help, too."

Kate took a small sip of water. It wasn't nearly enough to quench her thirst, but she didn't know how long she'd have to make her small supply last. The same with her food. She broke a piece of beef jerky in half then stowed the rest in her backpack and thought about the problem. She knew what lay behind. A monster who had already murdered two girls.

And though she didn't know exactly what lay ahead, she knew there was an occasional cabin in the wilderness, mostly near one of the many lakes. And if she found the Superior Hiking Trail there would be outpost shelters.

As the dawn crept in, wind howled around her picking up speed, sending eddies of ground snow swirling round her.

"I'm tough. I'm strong. How hard can it be to find a trading post on the trail?"

Kate left another hanging branch to mark her trail then set off once more. The path was more overgrown and far more treacherous than the groomed trails Kate was accustomed to in cross country ski competition. Though she'd never been with her dad along the entire length of the Superior Hiking Trail, this was obviously not part of it. This trail had no markers. And the way some of the trees were scarred, it was obviously used by people on horses and snowmobiles, both forbidden on the Superior Hiking Trail.

Suddenly Kate came to a halt. The trail split in two directions. Had Betty mentioned that?

Doubt crept in while icy winds clawed at her. She wanted her mom and dad. She wanted her home and her fireplace. She wanted the creamed corn her mom had promised to make just for her and the comfort of Jefferson curled beside her. A tear escaped and froze on her eyelash.

Adapt. Coach's voice was as clear as if he were standing beside her. *A mentally tough runner adapts to every situation.*

The trail had become rockier than when Kate left Betty's house. She gathered stones and quickly made a cairn to mark the left fork in the trail. The pile of rocks blended in with the wilderness. Hopefully a madman bent on murder would never notice.

She listened for sounds of the snowmobile behind her. Jonathan was too weak-minded and cowardly to run after her. Hearing nothing but the wind in the trees, she followed her instincts and set off on the left fork.

"Run," she told herself. "Move. You can do this."

When she'd been a competitive runner, she'd done interval training, running interspersed with strength and endurance training with at least one day built in for rest. Weekends had been devoted to uphill training, brutal ten-mile climbs that left her leg muscles burning. Cross-country competition runs that exceeded twenty miles often left her feet bleeding. And still she'd run. And won.

Kate kept a steady pace. If she didn't see the store soon, she'd have to decide whether to retrace her steps and explore the other fork or keep moving forward.

There was a sharp curve ahead, barely visible in the swirling snow. Kate moved toward the center of the trail to run a tangent, and that's when she saw it—a huge wooden monstrosity erected on two timbers that rose in the pre-dawn gloom. A billboard.

Hope surged through her. She was too far away to read the lettering, but she knew it was the trading post Betty had told her about. It *had* to be.

Speeding up as much as she dared, Kate pressed forward. From the beginning she'd battled against the darkness and the dangers in an unfamiliar and barely visible trail. If she let herself get overheated in freezing temperatures, she would be chilled by her own sweat.

"Come on," she told herself. "You can do this, Kate. You *can*."

She paced herself, all her senses alert for the unexpected, a rock buried under snow that could send her sprawling and break a leg, an air pocket that could bring her down and twist an ankle, even a predator in the woods looking for one last tasty meal before the storm hit.

Focus! The Coach's yell echoed through her mind.

"I won't think about the storm."

She was close enough now to see the outline of the general store. Kate raced toward the gas pumps out front.

Wait!

Something was wrong. Their inner workings had been pulled out, and one of the hoses lay half buried under the snow. The pumps squatted like sawed-off robots in front of an abandoned general store.

The roof sagged and wind blew snow through an open front door. Obviously Betty didn't know. Was she getting senile or did she simply not keep up with what was going on around her?

Though the front of store had the look of long-neglect, there was still a small possibility that somebody lived in back. Maybe it was no longer worthwhile to operate a trading post on a trail that looked seldom used, but the owners couldn't afford to leave their adjoining apartment.

With renewed hope, Kate headed through the open door.

"Hello? Is anybody here?"

Her voice echoed in the silence. Ghostly shadows cast by empty racks and shelves crowded in on her. She pulled her flashlight out of the backpack and trained the light around. A rusted-out cash register from another era presided over the grimy wooden countertop, and a chair with a cane bottom shredded by animals sat nearby. Behind that was a wall-hung telephone.

Kate seized it and held the receiver to her ear. There was no dial tone, not a single thing to indicate she might find a connection to a life that was now so far out of reach it was nothing but a dream.

Still, she said, "Hello?" When there was no answer, she said it again, her voice breaking apart on a sob.

Stay strong, Coach urged.

"I won't cry," she said. "I am mentally tough."

If she gave in to defeat now, she might as well sit down in the relative warmth of the store and wait to die. Still, the terrors of the house and the harrowing escape through the freezing forest had taken a toll.

Kate hung up the phone then shut the door against the wind and sat in an uncluttered corner of the general store to lean against the wall. Warmth began to seep through her and her head began to droop.

She jerked upright, and shook herself. If he caught her asleep, she'd die like the other two girls.

CHAPTER SEVEN

7:00 a.m.

"JONATHAN! WAKE UP!"

He rolled over, pulling the covers over his head. Jonathan wasn't ready to wake up. He'd been dreaming about that luscious plum waiting for him upstairs when the old hag stomped inside and interrupted him. The things he had planned for Kate today made him giddy.

She'd already discovered the wedding dress. Oh yes, she had. Yesterday when he'd come up from the basement where he'd stashed her laptop and had that argument with his mother, he'd heard Kate exploring her new home. That room- -her room now, theirs later—was imprinted on his memory. He could tell by the direction of her footsteps when she'd opened the closet door and found the wedding dress. Her wedding dress.

It didn't take a genius to figure out her perfect size. He'd been corresponding with Kate on Facebook for months. Since shortly after the last girl didn't work out.

Frankie, he'd called himself, using the photograph of a redheaded, freckled faced farm girl wearing thick glasses. He'd found the picture in an advertisement for some low-class homemade jellies nobody ever heard of. Frankie was just the kind of nerdy, needy girl Kate gravitated toward.

Kate was a do-gooder. Privileged girls often were. Life had been easy for her and she wanted to share with the less fortunate.

"Get your lazy self out of that bed!" The wretched bag poked him with the business end of a mop. A wet mop. "We've got a job to do."

He wanted to roar out of the covers like a lion king and take her down with one swipe of his big paw. He could, too.

It had been so easy to knock Kate out of her chair last night when she wouldn't let him kiss her. She'd even had the audacity to slap him. And after all he'd done for her--talked his mother into letting him take the food, arranged ham sandwiches on the tray himself then given up his precious time watching the six o'clock news on TV so he could sit in front of that fake snow scene by the window and have supper with her.

The girl had a lot to learn about being a proper wife. And he intended to teach her before the wedding.

Betty poked him again with the mop.

He threw back the covers and leaped up, fists balled. "What do you want?"

She didn't back up an inch. The old biddy. It was her fault he didn't get to play with Kate. Her and her false sympathy for the girl, always sneaking around spying on him, foiling his plans.

"The girl's gone."

"What do you mean, gone?"

"She escaped sometime last night. I told you that girl was smarter than she looked."

Jonathan raced up the stairs without even bothering to put on his clothes. Sure enough, her door was open. The hairpin she'd used to pick the lock was lying on the floor.

He flung himself onto her bed and rooted under the covers as if he might find her wadded into a tiny ball.

"Kate! Kate!" The covers smelled like her—the citrus scent of her hair and the light floral perfume she wore on her wrists and behind her knees. He's sniffed them all, repeatedly, while she was sleeping off the drug he'd slipped into the coffee he gave her when he rescued her.

He'd rescued them all. It had been ridiculously easy. Just plant a fake detour sign in the right weather, at the right time, rig up a plank in the road with nails protruding, then wait for the college girls to fall into his trap. So what if he occasionally caught a logger or some fool tourist family. He just helped them change tires and sent them on their way.

"I told you she's not here." Betty stood in the doorway with her arms crossed over her sagging body. Her uncombed hair stuck out from her headscarf like straw. All she needed to be a witch was a pointy hat and a wart on her nose.

As they tromped back downstairs to the kitchen, Jonathan wished for the thousandth time that his daddy had taken him along when he ran away. He didn't remember much about Harvey Westberg—he'd been only four when his daddy left—but anything would be better than living under Betty's thumb.

"When did you discover she'd escaped?" he asked her.

"Just now. When I went upstairs to mop. I came straight to tell you."

Old biddy. Mopping at the crack of dawn. Still, if she hadn't, Jonathan wouldn't know his future bride was missing.

"She can't be far. She's helpless as a kitten."

"You've got it wrong. As usual. Helpless girls don't know how to pick a lock."

"Why would she leave with a storm coming?"

"Use your head, dummy."

"That little whack I gave her at supper was nothing more than a love pat."

"Idiot! If I hadn't pulled you off her last night after you sneaked back up here, she'd be filing rape charges. She's probably heading to the authorities right now to name you for attempted rape and kidnapping."

"She wouldn't do that. She loves me!"

"She loves Frankie, you fool. Have you told her you're her pathetic little Facebook friend?" He scratched his head. "I thought not. Get some clothes on and get out there and take care of her."

Betty pulled out a frying pan and threw in some bacon, going about her day like she hadn't just pronounced a death sentence on Jonathan's bride.

He saw his entire future crumbling. He'd spent months searching social media for somebody like Kate and then grooming her on Facebook. She was perfect wife material, smart and generous hearted and sweet tempered. A simple girl. She didn't spend all her time sharing every detail of her life on social media like some of them. That was one of the reasons he'd targeted her.

Her posts and photos were rare, a few shots of having pizza with friends, a cute picture of her with the family pet, a picture of her hiking with her dad. Kate was the kind of girl who'd take naturally to the simple life—living in the woods, cooking his meals, washing his clothes and meeting his every need. He'd even imagined the babies they'd have together, chubby little cherubs with his intelligence and good looks and her sweet, pliable nature.

Maybe he could change Betty's mind.

"She's not like the others. Kate's kind and sensible. I can bring her back, and you can talk her into seeing what a good life she'll have with us. She'll learn to love it here. I know she will."

"How long do you think you can keep that little college girl happy in the backwoods?"

"She loves nature. She's said so in her posts. Sweet little thing tags along behind her daddy all the time."

"Are you insane? Do you know who her mother is?"

"Some mealy-mouthed housewife who loves dogs. Kate doesn't talk about her much on social media."

"She's a search and rescue handler, you fool!"

"How do you know?"

"I did an online search last night after I dragged your sorry self out of her room. You really hit the jackpot this time! If Maggie Carter finds that girl alive to tell her story, she's going to hunt you down like an animal. We'll both spend the rest of our lives behind bars."

Jonathan could feel the blood draining from his face. Betty was right. The old battle ax was always right.

"I don't know which direction to hunt for her."

"When I went out this morning to get the paper, I saw tracks going off toward the trail in the woods. Looks like she's heading toward that abandoned trading post. Nothing out there but wilderness."

Jonathan glanced toward the window. The sun was barely up and it would be freezing cold out there. He'd have to take a leak at least once before he got to that old wilderness trading post. He despised the idea of watching his own bodily fluids turning to icicles. And who was to say she'd be there anyway?

"That helpless little thing won't survive the wilderness. And even if she does, the storm's going to get her."

"That's not a risk I'm willing to take." Betty stomped to the coffee pot and poured herself a cup. "Get out there and take care of her the way you did the others."

He stormed back to his room and jerked on his clothes. But he had no intention of following orders. He didn't care what the old biddy said. Kate was different. And he was a grown man. He ought to be able to make his own decisions. If the old witch wasn't careful, he'd leave her just like his daddy had.

He grabbed his bow and quiver of arrows then climbed on his snowmobile and waved at her standing in the doorway, watching. Always watching.

"Take care of her. You hear me, Jonathan?"

"I will."

No sense arguing with the old fool. He'd learned a long time ago he could never win a war of words with Betty.

He headed into the woods and stayed on the trail till he rounded a corner out of her sight. Then he veered north in the direction of the truck stop. Kate wouldn't get far on foot in the snow, especially without her winter coat.

He'd have some breakfast then figure out what he was going to do with his future bride once he found her. One thing was for sure; he wouldn't take her back to the farmhouse where Betty would have her nose stuck into his business.

CHAPTER EIGHT

7:45 a.m.

JOE'S first glimpse of his daughter's wrecked car made him sick again. He turned from Maggie and sucked in the frigid air. No matter what the state of his crumbling marriage, he had to be strong for her while she worked with Jefferson, strong for his daughter.

"Maggie. Joe." Detective Roger Dillard strode toward them as they approached the wreckage, his bushy black hair pushing his cap upward so it sat on his head like a mushroom. His face was filled with concern. He'd known Kate since she was baby. He and his wife Claire were like second parents to her. "We've found her phone."

"Where?" Hope surged through Joe.

"At a truck stop in Toronto."

He glanced at his wife. Maggie was struggling with the same mixed emotions he had, despair, fear and a Herculean effort to cling to any shred of good news.

"What about Kate?" Maggie asked.

"She's not there. The trucker swears he never saw any girls fitting her description. He also swears he doesn't know how the phone got into his truck."

"Do you believe that?" Joe didn't. "My daughter's phone didn't get into his truck all by itself."

"The authorities in Toronto believe he's telling the truth. They did a thorough search of his truck and found no trace of Kate except for her cell phone."

"Just because the trucker didn't have my daughter..." Maggie choked up and turned away to control herself.

"Maggie's right, Roger. On what basis did they eliminate him as a suspect?"

"They've still got him for questioning. He has volunteered to call his trucking buddies on his CB and see if they saw anything on the stops he made on his long haul from the U.S. to Canada."

"And where was that?" Maggie said.

She now seemed fully composed but Joe knew better. His wife always internalized her missions. He'd watched her turn her heart inside out every time she searched for the lost. Most SAR handlers struggled to keep their emotions locked up, but both Joe and Maggie had found it impossible, particularly if the victim was a child.

The search for their own child had turned both of them into a walking bundle of nerves with one barely beating heart. Digging even deeper, Joe realized this was the first time he'd felt so close to Maggie in years. And that was a horror, all by itself, that it took a heinous act against his own flesh and blood to resurrect his emotions.

"The last two stops were in Chicago and Detroit," Roger said. "The first was at a truck stop north of here. I'm heading that way to ask some questions."

"Meantime, Kate could be anywhere," Joe said.

Maggie didn't wait around to hear Roger say, "We can't rule that out." She strode toward the truck, shouldered her backpack then let Jefferson out and hooked up his leash.

The big Lab went straight to their daughter's car and began circling it, his alert behavior that indicated Kate's scent was strong.

"Joe," Maggie called.

He gave his wife a thumbs-up signal. "She's set, Roger, and we've got less than seven hours to find our daughter."

While Maggie let Jefferson continue his search around the car, Joe gathered his large backpack that held the bulk of their supplies then made arrangements to stay in touch with the detective via two-way radio.

The Superior wilderness loomed in front of him, a beautiful place to admire nature when the weather was tame--a brutal place to survive when the weather turned so dangerous that even the most skilled outdoorsman might not survive.

He glanced at his watch. Eight o'clock. Only six and half hours until the storm hit, if the weatherman was right. Storms changed directions, shifted, lost steam or picked up intensity. The one constant of nature was its unpredictability. Even the most sophisticated tracking tools couldn't be a hundred percent sure what Holly would do next.

Kate had already been missing for twenty hours. The task of finding her, even with the best SAR dog in the U.S., was so daunting Joe felt as if his backpack weighed a thousand pounds. Every step he took might be his last. He might crumple to the ground, useless.

And hadn't he been useless now for several years, drifting through his life like a sleepwalker, aimless and unaware?

"Joe?" Maggie touched his shoulder, and he tired to shake off his ridiculous and untimely introspection. "Jefferson is raring to go. She's around here somewhere. I know it."

Maggie was right. An air scent dog never lied. And the big Lab had his nose turned straight toward the deep woods.

"Let's go," he said, and Maggie took Jefferson off the lead. The Lab raced off at a pace that buoyed his hope.

Air scent dogs search best in the early morning and late evening when the heavier air keeps a person's scent trail closer to the ground. It was barely an hour after sunrise and Jefferson already had a strong scent trail.

Jefferson barreled straight into the wilderness, setting a rapid pace. Within minutes they were out of sight of the wreckage. In the distance they could hear Roger's search party tearing through the woods, calling Kate's name. But as hard as he listened, Joe never heard the shout he wanted. *We've found her!*

Soon Jefferson was loping off toward an area Joe remembered from a trail he'd once scouted. If memory served, there had once been an old farmhouse in the vicinity, easily reachable by snowmobile. But on foot, even moving as rapidly as they were, it would be at least another couple of hours.

Last night's heavy ground snow was already airborne, hampering visibility. It would only get worse. How much conditions would deteriorate, and how rapidly, Joe could only guess.

Maggie had moved ahead with Jefferson so he stopped to catch his breath and study the weather. Portions of the sky were still a startling and burning blue. Nothing foreboding. Nothing to say that his daughter had vanished somewhere in the vast Superior wilderness and he might never find her alive.

His two-way radio crackled and Maggie's voice came through.

"Joe? Are you okay?"

"Yeah. Just studying the weather. You got something?"

"No. I was worried about you. Do you want me to wait?"

"No. Keep going. I'm following your trail."

The radio went silent, but something she'd said echoed in Joe's mind, *I was worried about you.* Over and over it played, like a record stuck in one groove—or the hint of a promise you never thought you'd hear.

CHAPTER NINE

8:20 A.M

WHEN THE LAW WALKED IN, Jonathan was at his favorite corner booth in the Glen's Crossing Truck Stop five miles north of where he'd lured Kate into her trap, enjoying his second order of pancakes with sausages and his third cup of coffee. It wasn't unusual to see cops coming in here for coffee and doughnuts, but this one, a tall, burly man with black bushy hair and the build of a linebacker, didn't order coffee. He started talking to the cashier.

When she hurried off toward the manager's office in back, Jonathan felt the first twinges of alarm.

The manager, Ricky Gerard, was a no-nonsense man who minded his own business. Still, when Ricky came out and started talking to the cop, every one of Jonathan's senses went on alert. He'd been here yesterday morning after he took Kate, trying to cover his tracks. He threw some money on the table then sauntered to the cigarette rack close enough to eavesdrop.

"Have you ever seen this girl?" The cop pulled a picture from his pocket and showed it to Ricky.

"Can't say that I have."

"She's tall, blond, blue eyes. Name's Kate Carter."

Jonathan eased to the other side of the rack so his back was to them.

She'd been covered with a tarp, and he'd parked the snowmobile out of range of security cameras and prying eyes. But could the wind have whipped it aside? Had someone glanced her way and seen her face?

"Ever hear anyone mention her by name?"

Jonathan tried to remember if he'd ever let it slip. He loved saying her name, loved the sound of it in his mouth, like strawberry ice cream. Before he grabbed her, he used to walk about the house saying her name aloud, "Kate, Kate, Kate." Finally Betty made him stop.

"No," Ricky told the cop. "Not that I recall. But then my memory's not as good as it used to be."

"Yesterday morning a trucker by the name of Jerry Harris saw a man he described as six feet tall, about two hundred pounds wearing a black ski cap and black parka messing around a Northwest America/Canada Transport." That stupid cop just wouldn't quit. "Do you know anybody who fits that description?"

Jonathan felt like a rat trapped in a maze. The only good thing is that today his ski cap was green. Still, if he ran, he might as well put a sign on his back that said *catch me if you can*. But if he stayed too long, the cop was bound to notice that he fit the description.

"You've just described about a dozen of my regulars. And I can't tell you which one. I never pay attention to what they're wearing."

"I need to take a look at your security tapes."

"Sure. Right this way."

Jonathan made himself wait until the cop was in the back before he got out of there. As he loped toward his snowmobile he glanced around the parking lot, trying to recreate yesterday morning's scene.

The Northwest America/Canada Transport had been parked close to the toilets with the passenger side away from security cameras. Stupid trucker had raced into the toilets and left his doors unlocked. Jonathan had parked his snowmobile on the far edge of the parking lot where tarmac met forest. It was practically unnoticeable in the shadows of overhanging branches and the deep shade of thick trees.

And Kate was passed out from the date-rape drug. No chance of her rousing from under the tarp to attract anybody's attention. Also chances of anybody looking under the tarp were slim to none. Folks in Minnesota minded their own business.

He'd counted on that when he sauntered toward the truck, not too fast, not too slow. He made no moves to attract attention, not even glancing around for watchers. That was a sure way to look guilty.

He'd been quick, too. Open the truck door like he owned it, toss Kate's cell phone under the seat and be on his way. He'd walked on like he was heading in for coffee then circled behind the building, keeping out of camera range, and climbed back onto his snowmobile.

Deed done. Jonathan had chuckled all the way home.

Judging from the way that cop was nosing around, Kate's GPS tracker had led them on a wild goose chase. Probably all the way to Canada.

Only problem was, somebody had seen him. Another trucker. Could have been somebody just pulling into the truck stop. Yesterday there had been only one truck on the lot when he'd parked the snowmobile.

And now the cop was too close for comfort. If the law got

lucky, they might find Kate before he did. And what about Kate's stupid mother with her search dog? Where was she?

That old bag had been right all along. He should have gone straight into the woods after his bride.

He headed south on the main roads, taking the shorter route home. Five miles from the truck stop he came upon Glen's Crossing Road where he'd taken Kate. Her car had been pulled out of the small ravine, the wrecker was still there and cops were everywhere.

Jonathan shot past Glen's Crossing then turned left onto a gravel road that eventually intersected the trail to Wayne's Trading Post. Adrenaline shot through him as he raced through the woods. The thought of losing her made him furious. And reckless. He almost overturned his snowmobile taking a curve too fast.

And of all the stupid things, he had to take a leak. He'd had too much coffee. And no time to go to the bathroom. Stupid cop.

He slammed on the brakes and leaped off, roaring her name out of sheer frustration.

"KATE! KATE!"

The icy wind bit his bare skin and took his breath away. He couldn't wait to zip up and be on his way.

Finally he was back on his snowmobile, racing off in the direction of that old falling-down store. She wouldn't leave the trail. Scared little girl like her. He'd find her first. He had to.

But with the cops after him, he had to come up with an entirely different plan. It wasn't enough to grab Kate and find some nice safe motel where he could tame her and house break her any way he pleased away from Betty's prying eyes. He had to hide her where nobody could find her.

Or else, kill her like he had the others and then go home, play innocent and let Betty be his alibi.

"KATE!" he screamed. "I'M COMING!"

GRAND MARSAIS 9 NEWS

Stan polished off another doughnut and topped off his coffee cup. He was on a caffeine and sugar high. They kept a fresh pot brewing at Channel 9 at all times and an endless supply of doughnuts of every variety. His favorites were the cream filled. He could eat his weight in them. And had today.

Doughnuts were such a welcome relief. Jean was on a health kick and lately all she'd served were salads, an endless parade of greens with weird ingredients like tofu.

The only reason he wasn't fifty pounds overweight is that he was only at the station for extended periods when storms like Holly made it necessary for him to stay at the station to give live updates.

His cell phone rang. It was his wife.

"Stanley?" He could already tell that she was beside herself. He chose to blame it on her pregnancy, her first. But he had a sneaking suspicion he was married to a woman who had inherited her Southern momma's flair for drama. "Can you come home?"

"No. I already told you that."

"Mother is crying that Christmas is ruined because the

flight was cancelled and she didn't even put up a tree, and Daddy can't do a thing with her. I'm pulling my hair out dealing with them and wondering what to do with all this food."

"Jean, they're grown. They can handle this little setback. I'm down here saving lives."

"Stanley should I go ahead and cook this food or freeze it?"

How should he know? He was a weatherman, for Pete's sake, not some stupid Master Chef like the guy Jean had been dating before Stanley stole her away. "Do what you think best, hon. I'm on in five. Gotta go."

He was more than happy to escape her and face the cameras, even with such dastardly weather news.

He dusted the sugar off his face then took his place in front of the cameras and put on his game face.

"A monster blizzard is heading our way, and her name is Holly. She's picking up speed and gathering force. Grand Marsais is expected to feel her full force as early a 1:30 this afternoon. I repeat, expect the snowstorm to hit at 1:30. "

He moved his pointer over the map as he talked. "We're already feeling Holly's effects with wind gusts up to twenty miles an hour. Temperatures are hovering at minus ten degrees and plunging rapidly."

The map behind him showed the temperatures in Grand Marsais, Glen's Crossing, Duluth and other key cities throughout the state, most of them sub-zero.

"Sustained winds of forty-five miles an hour with gusts up to seventy-five miles an hour will pose a huge danger, especially along our waterfronts. We're looking for a repeat of the winter storm that pushed ice and spray from Lake Superior into Duluth Harbor, freezing the spray within minutes and turning the harbor into a frozen tundra. The Land of Ten Thousand Lakes will be especially susceptible to these high winds and icy temperatures. Residents near lakes are advised to evacuate."

Stan had swallowed his last doughnut in haste and could feel the awful urge to burp.

"Stay tuned for weather updates here at TV 9 new in Grand Marsais."

He was relieved he'd held his gas long enough to get off camera. He pulled his handkerchief out of his pocket and mopped his brow, then went in search of something more substantial than doughnuts. A hotdog would do nicely.

CHAPTER TEN

9:00 a.m.

SOMETHING roared through Kate's dreams, startling her into a state of half wakefulness. What was it? The storm?

"Mom? Dad?"

There was no answer and she sat straight up, panicked. She wasn't in her room back home. She'd fallen asleep in the wreckage of an abandoned trading post in the middle of the wilderness. A quick glance at her watch told her she'd been asleep for more than two hours.

The distant roar became louder, unmistakably the sound of a snowmobile.

No, no, no, no, no...

Jonathan!

No doubt about it. Who else would be in the wilderness with a storm heading this way? The madman was on her trail. And she had no place to hide.

She was trapped in this forsaken, falling-down building like a mouse in a maze.

"Think." The sound of her own voice brought her out of her panic.

Moving as fast as she could, Kate pulled her lucky buckeye out of her backpack and tossed it into the corner. Even if he found it first, he wouldn't connect it with her.

But if her parents found it, they'd know what it was. Gran had given it to her for luck on her sixteenth birthday. An old Carter family tradition, she'd said. Kate carried it with her everywhere. Her lucky buckeye would scream to her parents, *I'm alive. I've been here. Don't give up. Come find me.*

She fastened on her snowshoes and gathered her belongings. In a split second she rejected the front of the trading post as an escape route. If he came into view before she got across the open space she'd be an easy target.

Would he shoot her? Or send an arrow straight through her heart? Had he killed the other girls first or dragged them back to that awful house to torture until he grew tired of them?

Panic obscured her vision as she thrashed blindly toward the back, crashing into abandoned furniture and knocking over a stack of empty boxes.

Stop, she could almost hear Coach saying. *Be tough.*

The voice in her head centered her and Kate made herself deep breathe, forced herself to assess the problem. There was a door at the back with rusty hinges, but she'd left tracks that would lead right up to it.

She whipped one of the stolen sweaters out of her backpack then raced through the store, dragging it through the dust. By the time she'd backtracked to the door, still dragging, it appeared a long-tailed animal of some kind had been in the store.

Satisfied, Kate stuffed the sweater into her pack and jerked on the door handle. It didn't move.

Please, please, please.

She centered herself then tugged with all her strength. Slowly, the door creaked open. Kate nearly cried with relief. Gran would say her guardian angels were with her. Gran would say, *There's no such thing as luck, Kate. Use your head, make smart decisions and live right, and your guardian angels will come when you need them.*

Kate plunged through and the wind hit her with a force that knocked her backward. The sound of the snowmobile was getting louder. Jonathan was closing in.

She righted herself and searched for the best escape route. Nothing was familiar to her. But she knew the Superior wilderness was filled with ridges and boulders, both of which would offer shelter and loose rocks she could use as weapons.

If she could get high enough, Jonathan would have to abandon his snowmobile and track her on foot. A real advantage.

As she climbed, heavy winds lifted curtains of snow off the ground and swirled it around her. Still, it wasn't enough to hide her escape route. Kate broke off a long branch and used it to sweep over her tracks.

"KATE!" His scream sent a chill through her.

"Don't let fear make you stupid," she told herself.

She kept climbing, kept covering her tracks. Move. Sweep. Move. Sweep. Kate lost herself in the rhythm, blocking out the new and horrifying threats as Jonathan came closer.

"You can't hide from me," he screeched. "I'm never going to let you get away!"

How close was he now? The rocks were larger at this elevation, and Kate searched for a hiding place.

"Please," she said.

That's when she saw it, a boulder that made a natural wall. She headed in that direction.

"KATE! YOU'RE MINE!"

She ducked under the boulder's natural overhang, but even there she still felt exposed. As her tormentor came closer, she backed deeper into the overhang. Suddenly, she'd backed into the narrow opening of a small cave.

Perfect. Even if he found her, he couldn't get into the cave without going through her.

"I'M COMING FOR YOU! KATE? DO YOU HEAR ME?"

"Come on, you sucker." She dropped her backpack to the cave floor then unfastened the ice ax. "Take one step into this cave and I'll split your crazy head in half."

Her own bravado left her shaking. Could she defend herself? She wasn't a violent person. Nobody in her family was. Did she have what it takes to defend herself against a maniac in the wilderness who was determined to murder her in cold blood and then pose her like a bride?

The snowmobile's motor went silent. Kate peered from her hiding place toward the trading post below. She could barely see his outline as Jonathan stood at the broken gas pumps bellowing her name. It seemed to her there was a new level of rage in his voice, a killing rage.

"YOU CAN'T ESCAPE ME, KATE! I'LL HUNT YOU TO THE ENDS OF THE EARTH!"

He stood in the open beside the pumps for what seemed hours. When he finally disappeared into the store, Kate sank to the ground and reached for her thermos. One small sip of water. That's all she'd allow herself.

Her immediate problem wasn't thirst. It was escape.

She didn't know what lay above or on the other side of the ridge. But long hikes with her dad made it possible to imagine the terrain. The ridges and valleys made for a constant switch between climbing and descending.

While the monster was in the store, she could keep moving, keep putting distance between them and hope he stayed inside long enough for her to find another hiding place. Or she could stay put and hope that when he finally left the store he would never guess that she had left the trail and was going in another direction.

"Better to travel with a plan than run out of panic," she said.

Her courage shored up by her latest pep talk, Kate moved deeper into the shadows of her cave. Stopping at a point where she hoped she'd be safe, she took a wide stance and raised the ice ax.

CHAPTER ELEVEN

JONATHAN STOOD at the pumps and cursed the snow. Instinct and logic told him Kate would have gone inside to get out of the cold, but the ground squalls had covered any signs she'd even made it this far.

He shoved his way through the door.

"Where are you!"

Jonathan could smell her. Even among all the rat droppings and the years' accumulation of dust and mold, he could still pick up her scent, like fresh peaches and cream, like a citrus grove in Florida, like something delicious he wanted to subdue and then eat from one end to the other.

"Come out! I know you're in here."

She was good at hide and seek. Clever little thing. If the cops weren't breathing down his neck, he'd have fun playing this game with her.

He trotted over to the defunct telephone. Her fingerprints were still there in the dust. Had she really thought she could call out? Had she imagined she could ring up that silly mother of hers and say, "Come and get me, please. I'm lost in the woods."

A babe in the woods was more like it. Skinny little thing. She was as insubstantial as milkweed. And just as a pretty. He pictured his future bride in summer, standing in an open field attracting monarch butterflies.

He stalked toward the back bellowing her name. Fresh tracks in the dust told him an animal of some kind was in the store with him. A 'coon? A skunk?

He slipped an arrow into his bow and pulled back the string. The unlucky skunk who tried to spray him would end up as his doormat.

To his left was what appeared to be a storage room. Kate was so slender she could be hiding in any number of nooks and crannies. He began kicking over boxes, peering inside. He found nothing but rat droppings.

"Kate. Come on out. I'm through playing with you."

Not a sound, not even a whimper. Furious, Jonathan dropped his weapon and started kicking the boxes then stomping them flat. Let her see how she liked that. Maybe a few bruises would teach her a lesson. He kicked and stomped every box there, more furious by the minute.

When he finished he stood heaving, his hands balled into fist.

"You'd better show yourself, young lady. When I find you I'm going to teach you a lesson you won't soon forget."

He imagined his fists pummeling into her soft flesh, the surprise on her face, the terror, the way her skin would tear and her blood would spurt. It wasn't the way he'd imagined starting off with his latest bride, but he knew how to get the upper hand. He'd had to show Jennifer he was boss before she became compliant.

Jonathan had no intention of ending up with a wife as bossy as his mother.

Storming out of the storage room, he kicked and smashed his way through the rest of the store. By the time he'd finished his search and destroy mission, he was shaking with fury.

Where was she?

10:00 a.m.

Kate had been in the shelter of her cave for half an hour when she eased toward the opening so she could get a better view of the trading post below. She was tense from fear and holding onto the ice ax, and she desperately needed to use the bathroom.

When she saw Jonathan walk into view, she sucked in a deep breath. Was he planning to track her up the hill or to continue along the trail?

He stopped at the gas pumps then turned in her direction and shaded his eyes. He couldn't possibly see her in the shadow of a cave. Had he figured out she'd laid a false trail to the back door and escaped up the bluff?

"KATE!"

His bellow came to her on the wind. Was it her imagination or had it picked up speed again?

With one last scream, Jonathan strode toward his snowmobile and drove off down the trail.

Kate was shaking so hard she had to sit down. She huddled in the cave with her head resting in the crook of her arms until the sound of his snowmobile vanished into the distance. After she took care of nature, she planted another *I'm alive* treasure in the cave. Then she strapped her ice ax onto her backpack, clambered from under her boulder and moved higher up the ridge.

She was surrounded by wilderness as far as the eye could see. What appeared to be a vast winter wonderland of trees was actually terrain riddled with lakes and ridges, boulders and caves. Fishing cabins would be hidden among the trees and an occasional logging camp. And somewhere down there, the Superior Hiking Trail.

Kate reached into her backpack to retrieve her compass, trying to shut out the signs that the blizzard was getting closer.

Her compass was gone. Had he taken that too, or had she forgotten to pack it? Without it, she could only guess which way would lead her home. Betty had mentioned that Jonathan would drive the snowmobile into Glen's Crossing, so she knew she was still more than sixty miles south of Grand Marsais. It was impossible to get there before the storm.

By now her parents would be searching. But even with Jefferson, it would be a daunting task. Under other circumstances, Kate would head back toward the farmhouse, closer to her car, easier for them to find her, easier for her to find a road that led into Glen's Crossing, or another house.

Obviously Betty would be no help. She hadn't been able to prevent her deranged son from coming after her. And he would surely double back home when he discovered she wasn't on the trail. He'd want to be safe before the storm hit.

Kate shouldered her backpack and continued to climb. The top of the ridge offered a better view. She swept her gaze in every direction, searching for signs of human life.

Was that a cabin? Kate blinked against the snowy glare and looked again. The silvery glint was the frozen surface of a series of lakes, and nearby was a tiny clearing, barely discernable at this distance. Inside the clearing was a cabin.

Safety.

Though the cabin gave the illusion of being just beyond the ridge, Kate knew from experience it would be a much longer hike. With a blizzard on the way, it was highly unlikely anyone would be in the cabin getting ready to ice fish on the lakes.

Could she make it before the storm hit?

She mentally marked the spot and headed down the ridge. If she was right, and she'd seen those lakes before, the Superior Hiking Trail was closer than she'd imagined. Finding the trail would be almost as good as finding her compass. It would be almost like finding home. Sections of the trail passed through private property. If she could shelter in the cabin during the storm, she could find the Superior trail afterward and be on a known pathway to safety.

She entered an open meadow and picked her up pace.

Suddenly she heard the snowmobile. It was coming closer by the minute.

It was him.

She swung her gaze in all directions. No boulders. No caves. Nowhere to hide.

And he was headed back to get her.

CHAPTER TWELVE

THE FARMHOUSE LAY ABOUT two hundred feet ahead, surrounded by woods on all sides and accessible only through a narrow trail Jefferson had scouted for the last hour. Maggie's remarkable SAR dog was now circling, alert behavior that indicated Kate's scent was strong here.

Still, Joe's spirits fell. He'd hoped to find his daughter in that house. He'd hope to race inside and rescue her, no matter who got in his way. But SAR dogs don't lie. If Kate were in that house, Jefferson would give Maggie the find signal. He'd be barking, and jumping for joy if he'd found Kate alive. And God forbid, barking while sitting still if he'd found her dead.

Joe's radio crackled to life, and up ahead, his wife gave Jefferson the stay command.

"Any luck with your search?" It was Roger.

"Not yet, but Jefferson has led us to a remote farmhouse. His alert behavior indicates our daughter has been here."

Maggie had trotted back to stand beside him. True to Jefferson's training and his amazing ability to take every situation in stride, the chocolate Lab waited exactly where she had stopped him, looking as comfortable and relaxed as if he were lying in front of the big wood-burning heater at the trading post instead of in the midst of the snowy woods.

"Joe, it's okay to find out if they've seen her," Roger said. "But don't give any details."

"Certainly not."

Maggie moved so close, Joe could see how the wind had already chapped her face where her ski cap and mask had slipped sideways. He adjusted it with one hand, and when she flashed a smile he felt the years falling away. He saw her as she'd been twenty years ago, her long dark hair curling at the nape of her slender neck, big green eyes staring at him from a perfect, heart-shaped face.

He'd hoped his daughter would look exactly like her. Instead she got his blue eyes and blond hair. Fortunately the Nordic coloring that didn't let him blend in with any crowd was lovely on Kate.

His heart squeezed. *Please, God, let me find her alive.*

Maggie leaned toward the radio. "What have you got, Roger?"

"A tall, heavyset young man wearing a black parka and skull cap was seen at the Glen's Crossing Truck Stop tossing what we believe to be Kate's cell phone into the Northwest America/Canada Transport yesterday before lunch."

Joe's blood froze. His daughter had been kidnapped. *Their* daughter. He put one arm around Maggie.

"Who was it?" His wife couldn't keep the wobble out of her voice.

"I have the names of five possible suspects. I'll be following up, asking questions, getting search warrants if I need to. Let me know if you find out anything."

"We will." Joe gave Roger their location before signing off and then studied Maggie. "You okay?"

"Yes. Let's go."

She gave Jefferson the search command and they began to move once more toward the house.

It was a two-story in need of repair. Even the airborne eddies of snow couldn't camouflage the fact that the house needed a good coat of paint and the porch steps were falling down. Jefferson strained against the leash as Maggie entered the yard, and a chill ran through Joe.

Premonition? The weather?

A loose shutter on the second floor banged against the side of the house. And that's when he saw it. Bars across an upstairs window. He scanned the other windows that were visible. Only one was barred.

He hoped Maggie didn't see. It would rip her heart out.

"Joe?" She nodded in the direction of the upper story. "You see that?"

"I do. It's probably nothing. Big houses in remote areas like this often have several generations of family living together. Could be senile grandparents at risk of trying to climb out the window. Or a child's room."

She didn't say anything, but she didn't buy it, either. He could tell by her eyes. One blink. *I don't believe you.* A second. *But I'm not going to argue.*

Maggie used to be passionate about everything, being a SAR handler, being a wife, being a mother, being a good citizen who gave freely of her time for the betterment of her community. When did it disappear? Was he the cause?

"Joe?"

"What?"

"That's the second time I've called your name."

"Sorry. What is it?"

They were almost at the front door. And there wasn't a

single sign of life inside the house.

"Will you ask the questions?" Maggie said.

"Are you sure?"

"Positive. Knowing what I know, I don't think I'll be able to say anything without crying or shouting or hitting somebody. Just about anybody will do."

He squeezed her hand. "I've got this, Mags."

How long since he'd called her Mags? Since he'd felt anything with her except the need to apologize. Or disappear.

He skirted a rotting step and crossed the porch. The door had neither bell nor brass knocker. Joe balled his hand into a fist and pounded. He thought he heard a scurrying, like house slippers sliding across a wooden floor.

He knocked again.

<hr>

BETTY's worst nightmare was standing on her front porch. The mother. Maggie Carter.

And that big dog. A hundred and thirty pounds if he was an ounce. Shiny coat all decked out in his Search and Rescue vest and harness. Fierce looking. A chocolate Labrador retriever, according to the information she'd found on the internet. Not like the black Labs she'd seen around here. They looked like they would lick you to death. This one was bigger and meaner. He looked like he could take you down in two seconds flat then rip you in half with one slash of his powerful jaws.

The man who was with them knocked on her door again.

She dropped the edge of the curtain where she'd been peering out and balled her fists in fury. That fool son of hers should have been back hours ago. How long did it take to hunt down a skinny college girl exhausted from floundering around in the woods and put her out of her misery?

He was weak, just like his daddy. It was just like Jonathan to leave her to clean up his messes. She'd let him have it when he got back. He'd think twice before he trolled around online looking for another bride.

The very idea. After she'd raised him and coddled him and given him everything he ever wanted, this was the way he repaid her. By trying to replace her. With three skinny, wimpy women who wouldn't hold a candle to her. No, they would not. In her prime Betty had been a golden goddess. She was still an imposing beauty when she wanted to be.

The man pounded her door again like he meant business. And that woman for sure was not going to give up and just walk away. Besides, Betty didn't want them to think nobody was home so they'd be free to just go nosing all over her property. She'd read that dogs like the brute standing on her porch could smell a body buried a mile underground.

"Just a minute." She made herself sound weak, and even added a big whooping, coughing fit for good measure.

Then she scampered into the hall bathroom to swab her throat and nose with Vick's salve. On second thought she socked herself in the nose with a full can of hair spray so it would be red and swollen. On the way back to the front door, she grabbed a shawl off the hall tree and swaddled herself.

She took her time opening the door, too. Let them stand out there and freeze. Maybe they'd think twice before they'd raise another daughter who went about luring nice young men like her son with their feminine wiles and their flirty ways and their perfumed hair.

That first one had been such a wily thing she'd even fooled Betty for a while. She'd put up with the girl for six weeks--and all that went on in that upstairs bedroom. After the foolish girl got pregnant, Betty had been forced to use her entire repertoire of manipulative skills on Jonathan. She told him she'd heard Jennifer sneaking out at night and he'd never know if he was the real father of her baby.

She'd vowed never to go through that again. And she hadn't. Not with the second girl, and not with Kate. Get them out of her house and get it over with--that was her motto.

When Betty finally opened the door just barely wide enough for them to see, she went into a coughing fit that spewed spittle everywhere. They jumped back like she'd used a cattle prod. It was all she could do to keep from laughing.

"I'm sick as a dog in here," she said. "Been like this for eight days. I'm so weak I can barely stand."

She could see sympathy building on the man's face, but Maggie Carter didn't buy her act. It was all because of that dog. No telling what he smelled around here. Yesterday morning when Jonathan had brought the girl in, she'd found the tarp wadded in the corner of the front porch. Stupid fool. She'd had to personally fold it back up and take it to that junky old shed out back.

"We're looking for our daughter." The man's hand was steady as a rock when he held out a picture of Kate. It appeared to be a high school graduation picture and it didn't do her justice. There'd been something about that girl, some tough inner fiber Betty could have admired if she hadn't been such a threat.

"I've never seen her."

"Her car went off the road on Glen's Crossing near here," he said. "Do you know anybody who saw the accident?"

"No," she said, and Maggie Carter made a sound like a mama grizzly bear about to rip your throat out. Let her growl. Betty didn't care. She wasn't about to tell them a thing.

"Is there anybody else in the house we could talk to?" Maggie Carter was a pushy woman. What she didn't know was that she'd met her match.

Betty covered her laughter with another coughing fit. For good measure, she lifted the end of her shawl and gave a big, honking imitation of blowing her nose. The nosey woman on the porch tightened her jaw and stuck out her chin.

Just let her try to get the best of Betty. She'd live to regret it.

"My son's upstairs sicker than I am. Poor little kid." She was proud of herself for that touch. It implied Jonathan might be seven or eight years old. No more than ten. Besides, if he needed an alibi, she'd already framed it. "He's got allergies, too. I hate to think what's going to happen to him when I go upstairs carrying that dog's scent with me. He's liable to pass out."

She didn't care who was standing on her porch. Nobody got the best of her.

"I'm sorry," the man said. Kate's daddy had her coloring and the same nose. It was small, aristocratic, and made him too handsome for his own good.

"Do you mind..."

"I mind everything," Betty said, cutting the Carter woman off. "I mind having to stand here in the freezing weather talking. I mind two strangers on my front porch. And I especially mind that you're on my property. Last year I had a break-in, and I still suffer anxiety attacks just thinking about it."

The man apologized again, but the woman looked like she might haul off and sock Betty in her already red and now throbbing nose. She wished she hadn't hit herself quite so hard.

"I don't plan to keep standing here in the weather and die of pneumonia. Leave now. And get that dog off my property."

The woman looked like she was going to argue, but the man took her arm and led her off the porch. Betty stood there glaring at them as they left. Let them turn around and get a good look at that. Her expression ought to scare them enough to stay away.

It looked like they were heading back where they came from.

"Ha!" Betty whispered. "Some search dog."

But then he veered toward the shed. Betty thought she'd die on the spot. But not from pneumonia. She was torn between racing outside with her shotgun or calling to warn her son. She was about to grab her gun and head outside when she saw the dog streak around the corner of the shed toward the trail in the woods. Both the Carters raced after him.

Betty threw off the shawl and kicked it into the corner while she searched her pocket for her cell phone. Where on earth had she put it?

She'd been in the kitchen when the nosey Carters came. She raced in that direction and tore up the place looking for it. She finally found it in the breadbox.

Those three girls had just about driven her crazy. If Jonathan brought another one here, Betty, herself, would put her out of her misery.

Don't think she couldn't, either. She was an expert with guns. Ask anybody, her son or even that useless ex-husband if you could find him. Betty was an expert marksman. During their brief marriage, she'd put more wild game on the table than he had.

She jerked her phone out of the breadbox and called her son. It went to voice mail.

"Jonathan? Are you there...? If you're deliberately not answering your phone just because it's me, then you're dumber than I thought. And that's saying a mouthful. You'd better take care of business and get out of the woods. Maggie Carter's after you with her search dog, and she's mad enough to spit fire."

CHAPTER THIRTEEN

THE OPEN MEADOW left Kate vulnerable, but it was the shortest route toward the lakes she'd seen from the bluff--and hopefully the cabin. Fighting against bitter winds and frigid temperatures she pushed forward. She was in full stride, going wide open when the arrow whizzed past her leg.

"STOP RIGHT THERE." Jonathan's yell spurred her on.

If he was trying to kill her, he'd completely missed the mark. Was he a bad shot or had he been trying to cripple her? Was his plan to bring her down like a wild animal on the run then overpower her and put a fatal arrow through her heart?

Think!

There, on the left. A copse of trees. Without breaking her stride Kate veered in that direction. It was quiet behind her now, but she didn't dare stop to look.

You can do this, Kate. In her mind, her coach was on the sidelines, urging her on as she raced toward the finish line. *You can do this. Keep on going.*

She was moving against the wind now, struggling as it buffeted her backwards, shivering as it moaned around her like something alive, like a new enemy that had risen from the earth. If Jonathan didn't get her first, the wind was determined to defeat her.

Stretch out! Push it!

With her coach's voice spurring her on, she pushed into the wind with all her strength, imagining herself on a groomed track in the spring, arms swinging, hips perfectly aligned under her shoulders. She made her steps quick, light, trying to increase stride turnover.

Run, Kate! You've got this.

The tree line loomed ahead, and suddenly she burst through. Cover. At last. Kate slowed, evened her breathing, listened for her killer.

Where was he? Why wasn't he pursuing her?

Ducking behind the trunk of a large spruce, Kate stopped to catch her breath and see what her enemy was doing.

He was barely visible through the curtain of snow. His snowmobile had come to a dead halt in the middle of the clearing. She didn't know if he was out of gas or out of a killing mood, but she wasn't about to wait around to find out.

She set off into the deep forest, constantly sweeping her gaze around for higher ground. She had to even the playing field. And that meant getting him off the snowmobile.

JONATHAN SAT on his snowmobile shaking with fury as he tapped Betty's name in his contact list.

"It's about time you called," she said. "Where are you?"

"You made me miss her!'

"What?"

"I had a clean shot at Kate, and you called right in the middle of it."

"She's not dead yet?"

"That's what I said. And it's all your fault."

"Well, excuse me for trying to keep you alive. Pardon me for being concerned about the safety of my own son. Listen up, stupid! Maggie Carter and her dog are in the woods hunting you down like an animal."

"The search dog's here?"

"That's what I said, moron."

"Don't call me that."

"Then don't act like one. What's taking you so long to kill the girl, anyhow?"

"She's smarter than I thought."

"I *told* you. You'd better take care of her soon. The latest weather report said the blizzard will be here around one-thirty."

"Wind's already blowing the ground snow so hard I can barely see."

"It'll be a whiteout soon. Take care of her and get home as fast as you can." Suddenly she said a string of words that even he wouldn't say.

"What?" he asked.

"Cops are on my porch."

"Don't tell them a thing."

"What do you think I am? An idiot? Unless they've got a warrant I'm not going to give them the time of day. I'm sick with the flu, and by the way, so are you. Upstairs in the bed."

Furious at the cops, his mother and his bride-to-be, Jonathan ended the call and screamed Kate's name. The answering silence mocked him. There was not a single sound in the wilderness except the moaning of the wind.

What did he think? That she'd answer?

She was nowhere in sight. Where did she go? For all the

good wondering would do, he might as well sit there and say eenie, meanie, minie, moe. Jonathan wasn't about to fail and let Betty keep rubbing it in about what a loser he was, a nincompoop, an incompetent fool. She'd called him every name in the book. Someday he was going to get a bellyful and show her who was boss.

Fury drove him to push the snowmobile to its limit. The wind got fiercer by the minute. Resulting snow squalls obscured his vision. Jonathan's snowmobile crashed so suddenly he barely had time to register that he'd slammed into a boulder.

He catapulted into the air, his arms and legs ricocheting like a rag doll. When his body slammed the ground, his right shin hit the boulder with a force that brought tears to his eyes. Jonathan sat there shaking his head in disbelief.

How did this happen? Luck was always on his side.

Until today.

Seething, he stood up and almost crumpled. His right leg was going to be bruised and sore for days. Maybe even broken. He tested his weight, and was surprised that it wasn't so bad. Bruised, maybe. Once he was riding again, he wouldn't be on it much anyway.

Still boiling at the injustice of his situation, he limped toward his snowmobile. It lay against the boulder like a dead bug. The front end was completely demolished, and parts of the machine lay scattered in the snow.

He was on foot now, and he hadn't even brought snow-shoes. Hadn't thought he'd need them. He was so hot with rage he almost forgot he was practically freezing to death. Kate's shenanigans were costing him the comforts of home in the storm—a big fire and a glass of whiskey.

The only good thing he could say about the situation was that his bow and quiver of arrows were still intact. Jonathan shouldered his weapon and limped toward the woods. He had to find a hiking stick, and he was going to find Kate. Make no mistake about it. If she thought he'd overlook what she'd put him through, she was sadly mistaken. Kate Carter was messing with the wrong man. And she would pay.

He entered the woods and began his search for a makeshift cane. He rejected several tree limbs that would be easy to cut with the knife he always carried. They weren't substantial enough to do the job.

His search brought him to the snowshoe tracks. Where in the world had they come from? Nobody was in this part of the woods with him except Kate. He'd have noticed. And she wasn't wearing snowshoes.

Jonathan knelt beside the tracks and looked in both directions. Clearly, they came from the area where he'd tried to cripple her with the arrow. And clearly, the clever girl had managed to find herself some snowshoes. But where? At the abandoned trading post?

Then he remembered the shed behind his house. Jonathan whipped out his phone and was about to tap Betty in his contacts when he remembered the cops on his porch.

He opened his mouth to yell out his frustration then stopped on a squeak.

That Carter woman was in the woods with her dog.

He tightened his jaws and gritted his teeth hard enough to crack enamel. He wanted to go home. He wanted to get into his bed and pull the covers over his head and forget he'd ever gone looking for a wife on the internet.

But if he didn't kill Kate, she'd tell. He was going to slaughter her like a deer.

The thought gave him a momentary burst of pleasure. Picturing the terror in her eyes and the thrill of watching her realize her fate, Jonathan whacked off the first branch that would do for a cane. Then he set off tracking his prey.

CHAPTER FOURTEEN

VISIBILITY WAS HORRIBLE, and Jefferson had gone full-out since they'd found the wreckage of Kate's car. He hadn't hesitated to press forward from the moment they hit the trail in the woods. Her scent had obviously been strong from the beginning.

When Jefferson went into alert shortly after they'd entered the woods, hope flooded through Maggie.

"Joe, look." She pointed to the broken branch then leaned down to praise her dog and to give him premium treats. He was expending enormous energy searching under these conditions. The treats would not only reward him, but help fuel and warm his body.

"Good girl!" Joe's face was filled with pride for their daughter as he strode over and inspected the branch. "The break's fresh."

"She's alive!"

"I think so, Mags."

She pounded his chest. "You *know* so, Joe! Jefferson alerted to her scent here. Our daughter's alive. Say it!"

"She's alive, and she's marking her trail." When her husband wrapped his arms around her, Maggie almost cried. How long had it been since he'd hugged her and meant it?

"Let's go then!" she said. There was no time to waste. That crazy woman at the house was hiding secrets, a killer either had her daughter or was stalking her, and the storm was closing in. "Jefferson, search."

The winds whipped up the ground snow, making the trail less visible by the minute. Still, when Jefferson alerted to the second broken branch, Maggie's heart soared. The mantra, *she's alive,* played through her, and she made outrageous promises to herself. When she got home with Kate, she'd do better. She'd talk to Joe about the things that really mattered.

It wasn't entirely his fault that they'd grown apart, far from it. She'd removed herself emotionally from her husband, kept secrets, hidden her own guilt. It had started when he left SARS and it had grown like cancer since then.

Up ahead Jefferson had stopped again. Maggie raced to catch up and when she saw why he'd alerted, her heart fell. Snowmobile tracks.

Joe caught up with her and stared at the deep groves in the snow.

"Jefferson caught his scent around her car, Joe. The monster's chasing her."

He caught her hand and squeezed. "God help him if he catches her."

"You're going to kill him?"

"No. Kate will."

Did her daughter have it in her to take the life of another, even if it meant kill or be killed? Maggie knew Kate was tough. Her athletic training had made her strong. And so had her heritage.

Maggie didn't hesitate to battle any kind of odds, plunge into any kind of weather, endure any kind of hardship to find the missing.

Once Joe had been like that. Was the man she'd married still in there somewhere? Was he in hiding, waiting for some sign from her to be resurrected?

As much as Maggie wanted to push forward, especially in light of finding the snowmobile tracks, she knew the folly of overheating her dog as well as Joe and herself.

"Stop," Maggie said. "Down." Her amazing dog immediately stretched out under the shelter of an overhanging fir tree.

Joe shrugged out of his backpack and poured Jefferson some water then brought the canteen over to share with Maggie.

"We'll have to make camp soon," he said.

"I know." Wind gusts were now so strong they bent the saplings nearly to the ground. She estimated they had barely more than an hour before whiteout conditions would put them all at risk.

"We'll find her." Joe caught for her hand and Maggie was surprised that he didn't let go. She looked at their gloved hands, joined, and wondered again, as she had a thousand times over the years, if their marriage would have stayed strong had Joe not left SAR. And yet, shouldn't a good marriage be about more than what kind of job you had?

A voice in her head said, *you know this is not about SAR,* but she quickly shut it down. The memories were too painful. Even after all these years.

The radio crackled and Roger came on.

"You two found anything yet?"

"Not yet," Maggie said, "but the scent trail is strong. What about you?"

"I got nothing from the woman at the farmhouse, Betty Westberg. But if she's sick I'm a walrus."

"That was my impression, too," Maggie said. "Did you get to talk to her son?"

"No. She told me the same story she told you. He's too sick to talk."

"Did you believe her?" Joe asked.

"No. After I left the Glen's Crossing Truck Stop, the owner called to say one of his waitresses remembered seeing Jonathan Westberg there yesterday morning. He didn't come inside like he usually does, but she swears she saw him in the parking lot."

As if Maggie weren't already cold enough, fear turned her blood to ice. Her daughter was out there in the wilderness and a maniac was hunting her down like an animal.

Joe gave her a concerned look but she just shook her head. She couldn't bear to think about the horror, let alone speak of it.

"Roger, did you find out what was in that shed?" he asked. "The broken window was fresh. Glass was still all over the ground."

"No. I didn't want to arouse the Westberg woman's suspicions. I'll have to go back out there with a search warrant."

"Jefferson was on full alert by the shed," Joe said. "I know they're hiding something."

"It'll have to wait. The latest reports say the storm will hit Grand Marsais around 1:30. It'll hit here earlier. You two should be setting up camp."

"We will."

Roger wished them good luck then signed off.

"Maggie. You okay?"

"I can't afford not to be, Joe." She stood up and dusted snow off her pants. "Let's get going."

They came upon the fork in the trail abruptly. Jefferson

immediately alerted to the cairn. Her daughter had not only made it this far, but she'd still been tough-minded enough to mark her trail.

That's my good girl. Way to go, Katie!

"She went in that direction, Maggie."

She didn't say, "I know." Her husband's face was filled with the kind of private hope she felt in her heart, and she gave him that moment.

As they followed her daughter's marker and her scent, she didn't have the heart to point out that so had the snowmobile. Joe had seen the tracks, of course. He was too smart not to.

He was walking beside her now, his arm linked through hers. Snow fell in increasing volume, wind howled around them and trees began to bend and crack. If they didn't make shelter soon, they'd get hit by a falling tree or be caught in the storm.

"Whiteout's coming, Mags. Call him in."

She could feel the tension in Joe. He'd been devastated when he lost Clint. Losing Jefferson might destroy him.

"Jefferson!" She couldn't even see her dog. Maggie called again, more urgent this time. She waited for a response, her heart pounding, while Joe squeezed her arm.

Suddenly he was streaking to them through clouds of snow that whirled like dervishes.

"Thank God," Joe muttered.

As she hooked up Jefferson's lead, praising him extravagantly, she thought about the deep pain Joe had kept inside all these years, and how it must have festered and grown until it left very little room for anything else. Especially a wife who still went blithely forth, taking her SAR dog into all sorts of dangers.

They moved forward and suddenly Joe shouted, "There!"

The building presented itself as no more than a shadow

until they got close enough to see the defunct gas tanks. Jefferson led them straight through the door.

Snow had already piled up inside and the dusty floor beyond was littered with tracks. Maggie took Jefferson off lead and he immediately began to scout.

"Joe? You see those tracks?" He was already taking off his backpack, and Maggie shed hers in the middle of the room.

"Yes." His face was tight with worry, and she couldn't bear to think what those large, man-sized footprints in the dust meant for her daughter.

Had blind luck led them there or divine intervention?

"We'll set up camp here," he added.

With a blizzard almost on them, there was nothing they could do about the tracks now.

The abandoned building was almost the perfect spot to shelter. The walls would block the storm and the floor would provide added insulation against the bottom of their popup winter tent. Camping here would save them at least an hour cutting branches and fashioning a lean-to against the natural wall of one of the many boulders in the wilderness. And it would provide far more protection.

Joe began to make camp while Maggie watered her dog again and filled his dog food bowl. Working under these conditions, Jefferson expended a tremendous amount of energy and dehydration was a real threat. Joe had packed enough water so that would not be a problem for a while, hopefully for the duration of the search. But if they ran out, he could always heat the snow to make it potable, though gathering enough would be a laborious process.

Maggie glanced out the window at the worsening conditions. Wind howled around the building and visibility was almost zero.

"Where are you, Kate?" she whispered. How could her daughter possibly survive this storm? Another thought pushed through, the one she'd locked deep inside. Was her daughter even still alive?

She was certain Kate had broken the branches and built the cairn. Since Jefferson's search was scent specific, so were his alerts. Still, anything could have happened between the time Kate marked her trail and Maggie found it. That maniac could have overtaken her on his snowmobile and killed her.

Or worse. Decided to torture her first, the way he had those other girls.

She felt helpless. How long would the blizzard keep them trapped here? Hours? Days?

"Maggie!" Joe's call brought her out of her dark and brooding mood. "Jefferson's got something."

Her dog was in the corner of the room circling with excitement. Maggie raced over to look. At first she saw nothing but a dirty, dark wooden floor. Then she spotted it. The dust on the floor had been disturbed and a tiny brown nut lay in the corner.

Kate's lucky buckeye. Maggie picked it up and clutched it to her breast as if she'd found her daughter.

"Maggie?"

"Look." She held the nut in her open palm. "She was here, Joe."

He wrapped her in his arms and buried his face in her hair. "Our daughter's alive, Mags."

They turned their backs to the storm outside and held onto each other. Simply held on.

CHAPTER FIFTEEN

12:05 p.m.

JONATHAN HAD LOST her tracks nearly an hour ago and his leg muscles burned like fire. Not to mention he was struggling for breath, his bruised leg was swollen, and he didn't know if he could take another step. He was furious and he didn't care who knew or heard.

"KATE! WHERE ARE YOU!"

The wind snatched his scream and tossed it into the mayhem of nature at its most dangerous. Treetops snapped with gun-shot cracks and giant trees groaned as their roots were lifted from the ground. An enormous fir crashed in front of him and he tumbled backward screeching with rage. The tree narrowly missed him.

Kate wouldn't live through this. She was probably lying in the snow right now, crushed under a tree. He hoped one the branches drove straight through her fickle heart.

He should have gone back home when he had the chance. He could have sneaked through the back way without being spotted by the cops. He could be sitting in the nook by the barred windows now, drinking hot chocolate and wolfing down roast beef sandwiches and thinking about the things he'd meant to do to Kate in that bed. Their bed.

He howled again, shaking his fists at the curtain of white that kept him from finding his prize. He'd already decided what he was going to do with her. He'd kill her, of course, but not before he'd satisfied his lust and his rage and his burning thirst for revenge.

He wanted to find her alive. He salivated at the idea.

Before the weather got so bad, he'd noticed she was heading toward the lakes. He knew the area, knew what was there. Could she have made it?

Another tree slammed to the forest floor, not ten feet away. He catapulted to his feet. He had to get moving. If he didn't, he was going to be killed by a falling tree or completely lost in a whiteout.

"KATE, I'M COMING! YOU'LL BE SORRY!"

KATE'S LEG muscles burned and she could barely see. The wind battered and screamed at her like something alive, like something that was determined to defeat her. If she didn't find the cabin soon, she'd never make it.

Keep going. Coach Lucas seemed so real she could almost see him.

She was transported back to a brisk fall day, beautiful weekend, golden leaves, light breeze, legs on fire, right foot bleeding. She was nine miles into her training climb and so ready to stop she could feel the relief of taking off her running shoes. She could taste the water waiting for her, the strawberry-banana sport drink.

"I can't."

The sunshine and autumn leaves dissolved and she was surrounded by a frozen world where everything had turned to ice and snow.

You can. Push through the pain.

With memories of her Coach's voice cheering her on, Kate pushed through, kept going. She was no longer even certain she was going in the right direction. She was getting dehydrated. She could hardly feel her feet and hands. Her water was almost gone. Her mind was getting fuzzy. She'd only glimpsed the cabin from afar when she was on the bluff. She didn't know whether she'd calculated the correct distance or whether the cabin was even there.

Maybe she was just going around in circles.

Lost people do.

Was that her mother? Was she here?

"Mom!" Kate's voice was borne off in gusts that blew her body sideways. Nobody answered when she called. Nobody came.

She was so tired. And so cold. What if she could just lie down for a minute to rest?

Don't give up, Kate! Coach Lucas was so real she could see the veins standing out on his neck. *Quitters don't win! Are you a quitter?*

"No."

Say it, Kate.

"I'm not a quitter."

But she had options. Keep going? Or try to dig a snow cave, wrap in her space blanket and sleep through it all?

But wait. That didn't sound right. Kate struggled to remember why and it finally hit her. Blizzards brought drifts as much as thirty feet high. She'd be buried alive.

Hesitation will make you lose.

Kate no longer knew if Coach Keith Lucas was with her in the wilderness or simply in her head.

"Coach? Where are you?"

Her steps slowed and she rubbed her forehead. "Think," she whispered. Her lips felt frozen, raw. Her voice was a hoarse croak. "Think."

Everywhere she looked was white, the snow, the forest, the sky, even her own body. Nothing but white. It mesmerized. Paralyzed.

What if she sat down for a while? Just one minute?

She felt her legs giving way, heard Coach scream, *Stop!*

Kate straightened up, dug deep into herself for the last ounce of courage.

You can do this, Kate. She pictured Coach there on the sidelines, as always, cheering her on.

Her instincts and her training took over and she ran, bleeding and freezing, hoping and praying... and determined.

"Today is not my day to die," she said.

She summoned up her last reserves of strength, called on that last burst of speed. The cabin materialized so quickly she stumbled and fell onto the porch.

She wanted to sit down right there and cry.

Don't you dare. Coach such a taskmaster, even in her imagination.

She'd been running and hiding for seven hours in a treacherous winter wilderness. She'd been dodging arrows and trying to outwit a cold-blooded murderer and outrun a storm since before dawn.

"Why?" She tried to scream at Coach, but it came out a squeak. "What else do you want?"

The phantom companion who had been with her throughout her ordeal in the wilderness didn't answer, and she struggled to gather her thoughts. Food. That's what she needed. Kate found the granola bar Betty had given her and wolfed it down.

A cracking sound exploded and a fir tree crashed onto the

end of the porch. Kate scrambled backward as the roof on the west end of the porch caved in. Falling debris rained around her and a porch beam narrowly missed her head as it crashed to the floor.

She had to get inside. It came to her with the same clarity she'd always felt during competition when the finish line was in sight and she knew exactly what to do.

No time to hunt for a key hidden outside. No time to see if she could jiggle a window loose from its lock so she could climb inside.

"I didn't come this far to die."

Filled with renewed determination, she untied her ice ax and bashed open the nearest window. Another quick swipe around the window frame, and she'd removed the shards and was inside the cabin.

The instant feeling of comfort made her weak-kneed. She dropped her backpack on the floor and sank onto a plaid sofa facing the cold fireplace. It was heaven to be out of the wind, to breathe without feeling as if ice were plunging through her lungs, to rest the muscles that had just passed the biggest endurance test of her life.

The race is not over, Kate.

"I know, Coach."

A killer was out there. And he was coming.

Her voice was still a hoarse croak. Kate dug into her backpack and pulled out her thermos. No need to parcel out the remains. The bottle was almost empty.

As she drank the last of the water, snow swirled through the broken window. Kate stuffed it with sofa pillows then pulled off her snowshoes, hiking boots, socks and damp snowsuit. There were blisters on her feet, and one of them was bleeding.

It was nothing compared to the cold. She put on two pairs

of wool socks she'd nabbed from Betty's shed and went in search of a blanket. She had to get her core warm.

The cabin was small--a front room with fireplace, sofa and table with chairs for four, a tiny bathroom with the water drained from the toilet and the pipes of a wall-hung sink and a shower, a small hall that led to a bedroom with one double bed piled high with blankets and a closet containing more. Kate wrapped herself in three blankets from the closet then stood there a while shivering.

"Just my body trying to restore itself to normal temperature," she said. "Now get moving."

She found a kitchen at the back of the cabin. It was hardly bigger than a galley.

Holding her blankets close, Kate started her search. Louvered doors at the end of the galley led to a compact washer and dryer complete with a shelf of laundry supplies. She started flinging open kitchen cabinets. She found dishes but no tins of canned food, no bags of rice and cereal to attract varmints. Not even a box of stale crackers. Not even a crumb.

Fighting against rising dismay, she flung open the last cabinet.

"Jackpot."

The shelves were stocked with cooking oil, vinegar, tea bags and various condiments along with stacks of freeze-dried meals, including her favorite, lasagna with meat sauce. Relief overwhelmed her, and she stood in front of the food battling back tears.

See, I told you your guardian angels would come. Her grand-mother's voice.

The pasta was exactly the fuel she needed after her grueling escape. She stuffed the pockets of Betty's jacket then went in search of water.

She found the gallon water jugs in the bottom cabinet

near the back door. Not surprisingly, the water was frozen solid.

A quick survey showed that the owners of this cabin had winterized the smart way. No pilot lights were left burning, not even in the water heater, which had been drained.

Kate searched all the drawers in the kitchen cabinet till she found matches and a screwdriver mixed in with an assortment of cutlery. She nabbed a spoon and the screwdriver and stuffed them in her pockets. If she had to leave here for any reason, she'd be a girl with tools.

But where was the wood? The wood basket beside the backdoor was empty. And there was no way Kate could go back into the storm to gather wood. Even if she could see to find it, it would be wet.

She balled her hands into fists. "I will not be defeated. I won't."

She'd escaped a maniac and was still alive to tell the tale. She wasn't going to curl up and die now. If she had to, she'd break the chairs apart with her ice ax and burn them in the fireplace.

She unlatched the door at the back of the kitchen and pushed it open. It led to a small enclosed porch that had been winterized. Shutters had been lowered over the screens and bits of snow filtered through. But in the corner, covered and kept dry by a tarp, was Kate's precious, life-saving wood.

Without wasting a moment, she filled her arms with fireplace logs and plenty of kindling then went back inside and set to work building her fire, never mind that she was dragging somebody else's blankets all over the floor. They'd just have to forgive her.

She dumped her wood by the fireplace then knelt in front of it. Years of hiking and camping had taught her how to build a fire, even the hard way if she didn't have matches.

Thankfully, the matches saved the day, and she soon had a

fire going. Her next order of business was to cut the ice chunks out of their plastic jugs with her ice ax then melt them for drinking and reconstituting her freeze-dried food.

It was almost like being ten years old again.

By the time she was drinking hot tea from a mug she'd found in the kitchen and stuffing herself with the pasta with meat sauce, the storm outside and the killer chasing her had receded. Even her shivering had stopped.

Kate was transported back in time. She became a little kid again, sitting in front of a blazing campfire watching her dad stir beef stew over the fire while her mom sat nearby strumming her guitar. Her SAR dog, a big golden retriever named Kelly, lay at her feet.

Her dad smiled at her. "This is the good life, isn't it, Katie bug?"

"It's cool."

"Do you want to roast marshmallows while the stew's cooking?"

She jumped up and ran to her dad, glad he wasn't like her best friend Sally's dad. He never took the time to do anything with Sally. Kate slid into her dad's lap and he took out his pocketknife and showed her how to trim the end of the roasting stick.

Her mom smiled at them. Most moms would say, "She's going to cut herself," but Kate's mother was always encouraging her to try new things.

Like so many others before it, that childhood camping trip had been great, and one the last times she'd seen her parents happy together.

Now Kate leaned closer to the fireplace, warmed by the crackling fire and her memories. What had happened between her parents to make it all go so wrong? They were both good people, and both of them loved her. Why did they no longer show that love to each other?

Was there anything she could do to help them get it back? If she got out of this mess--*when* she got out of this mess--she was going to ask questions, try to find answers.

Kate filled her thermos with water she'd thawed, then put the thermos and the freeze-dried dinners from her pockets into her backpack. Next she tided up, disposing of her teabag and freeze-dried dinner containers in a garbage bag, rinsing her cup with the leftover water and setting it in the sink to dry.

Her dad used to tell her, "Never camp with a messy roommate."

"Why?"

"You'll get bears in your tent."

The memory made her smile. She was still smiling as she added another log to the fire then pulled more blankets out of the bedroom closet and placed them by the fire.

The wind roared, beast-like, around the cabin and nothing was visible outside except a curtain of white. Still, Kate went to the window and stood there, searching, searching.

Had Jonathan continued to follow her? Or had he turned to go back home? Surely he was back in the farmhouse with Betty.

Poor woman. Would he take care of her through the storm or let her do all the work?

Kate had heard him yelling at his mother, calling her all kinds of foul names.

"Beast!" she said, then lowered the curtain, walked back to the fire and snuggled into her pile of blankets. She'd stay close during the storm. She still felt chilled from prolonged exposure, and didn't know how long it would take to feel as if she'd brought her body temperature back to normal.

The heat began to make her drowsy. To keep herself awake she ran through a list of things she planned to do. Her parents had given her everything, and she was going to make them proud. She was going to get through this ordeal and finish her degree in veterinary medicine. She was...

"KATE!"

She leaped to her feet.

The beast was back. And she had nowhere to run.

CHAPTER SIXTEEN

1:00 p.m.

OUTSIDE THE TRADING POST snowstorm Holly lashed out in full fury, shaking the rafters, battering the doors and windows, uprooting giant trees whose thunderous, dying gasps could be heard over the howling wind. Though it was early afternoon, the complete whiteout made the inside of the trading post gloomy.

Still, Joe could see how his wife shivered from the long exposure to sub-zero temperatures. It hurt that she no longer turned to him for warmth and comfort, and that it was no longer natural for him to offer.

"Go inside the tent, Mags." It went without saying that Jefferson would go, too. He was part of the family, and he would follow Maggie to the ends of the earth.

"She's out there, Joe."

"She's smart. She's sheltered somewhere. She knows how."

Maggie nodded. Probably too full of emotion to talk

about Kate anymore without crying. He was, too, and that was a fact.

"Are you coming?"

"I'll cook first. The stove will warm me up some."

The so-called stove was nothing more than a burner perched on a portable propane canister, the pocket rocket backpacking variety which set up quickly. He didn't cook much at home except for the occasional scrambled egg or grilled steak, but he enjoyed cooking when they camped.

Today being the notable exception. What was to enjoy about hunkering down in an abandoned building while your only child was lost in a blizzard?

Maggie stood watching him, her face unreadable, and then she ducked inside the tent with Jefferson following. They huddled together on the sleep pad he'd spread earlier, the big Lab leaning against her legs and her arms wrapped him. Was she only thinking of sharing Jefferson's body heat? Or was she thinking, as he did, that no manner of intelligence and know-how would be enough for Kate to survive this storm without supplies.

"Mags."

"Yeah?"

"Turn on the lantern."

It was the old Candoil backpacking lantern he'd bought many years ago when the outdoor equipment companies improved the candle burning lanterns. It provided both light and enough heat to add warmth to the inside of a tent, even in the worst winter weather.

"I know."

She got the lantern going and he could see them silhouetted through the canvas, a woman whose bond with her dog would never be broken, no matter what, a woman so committed to search and rescue missions, she was willing to put her own life on the line, over and over.

She'd even been willing to put your sons on the line.

The thought came unbidden, and Joe pushed it away. *Don't go there.*

But something had opened the floodgates--the search for his daughter, working the storm with Maggie and Jefferson, feeling a resurrection of the close bond they used to have working SAR missions.

He thought of *before,* of the last camping trip he'd taken when Kate was ten and he and Maggie had a real shot at recapturing the happiness they'd known before he lost Clint at the World Trade Towers. Maggie had been so happy then, playing the guitar that was now collecting dust in the back of the closet, sending him secret knowing smiles, occasionally running her hand over her still-flat abdomen.

Looking at her, you'd never know she was pregnant with twins. His sons. Joe had been beside himself with joy. The pregnancy changed everything, closed the distance he'd felt with his wife since 9-11, restored his dreams for a future of growing old with her, of watching their children grow up and go to college and marry and have kids.

The pregnancy was a miracle for them, an unexpected gift. Kate's eleventh birthday was only a few weeks away, and they'd planned to tell her then, together. "You're going to have two baby brothers," they'd say. They were even going to let her help choose the names.

Then Maggie got a call for a SAR mission. Two young girls missing from a youth camp in the Superior wilderness.

Their argument had been fierce.

"Let somebody else go, Mags."

"They're *ten,* Joe. And I might be their only hope for survival."

"You're not. There are other very capable SAR handlers."

"But I'm the closest. You know the sooner they are rescued the more likely they'll be alive."

"You'd risk our sons?" It was a low blow and he knew it. But he was filled with foreboding, desperate to keep her and his unborn babies safe.

Maggie's face turned white. "I'm pregnant, Joe, not infirm. There is no reason for me to stay home like a hothouse flower."

"You'll be going into an area where the terrain is particularly treacherous. It will be too risky, Maggie."

She'd covered her womb with both hands, a mother bear, fierce and protective. "Do you think I'd deliberately put my babies at risk? Is that what you think, Joe?"

"I don't know what to think anymore."

And there it was. The last bitter words he'd said before Maggie left on the mission. The accusation that must have been in her mind when she'd fallen and started bleeding, when she was airlifted out of the wilderness to the hospital where doctors told her there was nothing they could do. Her babies were gone, and she could never have another.

Afterward, neither of them talked about it, and Kate had never known. They moved forward as if nothing had happened, as if the hole left by two baby boys weren't getting bigger every day.

Now he glanced at his wife inside the tent. Her head was bowed. What was she thinking? Did she ever remember?

Joe took their meals off the burner then made coffee.

"Mags?" He had to call her name twice before she looked up. "Food's ready."

"I'm not hungry."

"You have to eat."

One of the best ways to warm the body was to fuel it with hot food and drink. She knew that better than anyone.

"I know."

She eased away from Jefferson, though he was sleeping so soundly he never stirred when she crawled from the tent.

Though their campsite was inside a building, Joe had set up the camping stove as far away from the tent as possible.

Kate used to giggle when he'd tell her that food, even crumbs, left inside the tent was a sure way to attract unwanted animal guests, including bears. "When you camp," he'd say, "never eat where you sleep."

Maggie sat on the other side of the burner and they both dug into their meals, eating in silence. It was like so many meals at home that Joe shouldn't even have noticed. For the first time in years he knew why Maggie was always saying to him, *we never talk.* For the first time since they'd lost their babies, he wanted to smash the silence with both fists.

But how to bring up a subject that had festered inside him for nine years? Instead he stowed their trash inside an odor proof bag then found a door at the back of the building. It took all his strength to open it against the storm, and then the wind snatched the door and almost tore it from the hinges. Joe had to hang onto the doorframe to keep from being sucked into the storm.

He was panting and shaking with cold when he finally managed to close the door. Joe dusted the snow off his clothes and made his way back to the front room.

His wife was still huddled over the burner, shivering again.

"Let's take our coffee inside, Mags.

Heat from the lantern and Jefferson's body made the inside of the tent a welcome relief. Still, Joe sat as close to Maggie as possible.

"How long do you think the storm will last?" she said.

"Hard to tell right now."

"She won't last days. Not without supplies."

"Kate's resourceful. Let's don't think otherwise, Mags."

Maggie sipped her coffee, nodding hard as if she were trying to convince herself. Then tears welled up and spilled over.

"It's my fault she's gone," she said.

"It's the fault of that depraved maniac who took her."

"If I'd let you go after her, none of this would have happened."

She was crying in earnest now. Joe set his coffee aside and pulled her close. Thankfully, she didn't pull away.

"Shh, Mags. You can't take this on yourself."

The guilt would destroy her. How many times through the years had he blamed himself for standing idly by while his pregnant wife went on a SAR mission into terrain he knew would be treacherous? Why hadn't he offered to take her dog and do the search, himself? He'd been there for most of her refresher training sessions at home with Kelly. He knew the commands and how the dog worked. The dog knew him—and was trained to work with other handlers if necessary.

"I'm sorry, Mags."

"What?" She sniffed and stared at him. "What are you talking about?"

"I'm sorry I haven't been there for you and Kate. I'm sorry I didn't insist on driving to the college to get her. Sorry I didn't take your place on that SAR mission nine years ago."

The shock of his admission showed on her face, on the way she went very still. Was she angry? Hurt? Wondering why he was talking about a subject that had been taboo for nearly half their marriage?

"Kelly would have worked with me. I should have gone instead of you."

"You couldn't have known what would happen, Joe."

"Neither could you."

"I blamed myself."

"I blamed you, too, for a while," he said. "But mostly I blamed myself."

"Why?"

"A man is supposed to protect those he loves. I didn't protect anybody, Mags, including you."

She snorted and scooted out of his embrace. "That's antiquated thinking, Joe Carter. I'm an independent woman. I don't need anybody to look after me. I take care of myself."

Was her feisty response a way of avoiding the hard truth? Or had she grown so far from him there was no going back?

Joe picked up his cup and sipped his coffee. It would easy to let the subject drop, easy to slide back into their routine of refusing to have any conversation with substance. The wind howled like a wild thing, and he felt as raw as the winter storm.

He also felt that this was his last chance to save his marriage. And it was slowly slipping away.

"I should have been more supportive of you when you lost the babies."

Her surprise showed on her face, on the way she studied him intently now, the way she appeared to be burrowing beneath his skin trying to peer straight into his soul.

"I thought you had closed yourself off because you hated me," she said.

"No. I hated myself."

"Oh, Joe. What a mess we've made of things." She leaned her head briefly against his shoulder, a very good sign. Still, you couldn't erase years in one vulnerable moment. You couldn't turn back the clock and redo everything that had gone before.

"I'd like to change things going forward, Mags, to try to make things good again."

"I don't know."

Three words. Joe could take them as a stake driven through his heart, or he could seize them as a shred of hope.

"I understand."

119

"Joe." She cupped his face, looked deep into his eyes. "I can't even think about the future until I find Kate."

"You don't have to, Mags. I'm here... I'll be here."

He started to add *always,* but he was afraid of sounding foolish, like some besotted wimp in those chick flick movies his daughter watched.

What was Kate doing now? She was tough, smart and supremely fit. But she was also young and vulnerable and scared and unequipped in the midst of one of the worst blizzards in Minnesota's history. If Joe thought about the possibilities he'd go crazy.

Instead he wrapped his arms around his wife, whispered, "Body heat," and prepared to wait out the storm.

CHAPTER SEVENTEEN

1:00 p.m.

JONATHAN WAS BEYOND HUNGER, cold and fatigue. He battled through the whiteout with one driving force. When this blizzard was over he was going to find the woman who had done this to him, and he was going to torture and kill her.

He screamed her name, fueled by rage. The blizzard wasn't going to get him. Nothing was going to get him before he made Kate pay for everything she'd done to him. No woman slapped him, rejected his advances then spurned the home he offered and lived to tell about it.

He stumbled over something in the snow. A rock, a root, a fallen tree? He couldn't tell until he landed on his bruised leg. There was something solid underneath. A floor! He reached blindly through the snow. A wall! A door!

Jonathan kicked it in with his good leg then stood, disoriented and disbelieving, blinking his frozen lashes. A log burned through, crackling as it shot sparks. The fire was not a hallucination. It was real.

Jonathan hurried to the blaze and squatted in front of it with his hands outstretched. Gradually his shivering calmed to a manageable level.

"Hello?" he called. "Is anybody home?"

He waited for the answer, swung his gaze to every corner of the room for some old codger to rise up out of his easy chair and offer him a cup of coffee. A warm blanket. Some ham and biscuit.

Jonathan was starving. He'd had nothing since breakfast that morning, and even two helpings of everything hadn't prepared him for stomping around in a blizzard looking for his bride.

His ex-bride, he reminded himself. She could be replaced as easily as the other two.

Easier than Jennifer. That's the one he'd debated with himself before killing. That's the one he'd almost let loose in the wilderness just to see if she'd live, just to see if she'd come crawling back to him.

She'd begged. She'd promised to be good, to do anything he wanted, any way he wanted it.

She even swore that he was the father of her baby.

Jennifer came to him as plainly as if she'd suddenly appeared in the cabin and was standing there all big-eyed and scared.

"I didn't sleep around," she said. "I swear to you."

"Don't lie to me. My mother saw you sneaking out."

"No! She's the one lying." While he positioned the arrow in his bow, she'd put her hands over her belly. "Please, please! Don't kill me! If you do the baby dies, too."

"Do you think I care about some other man's brat?"

He still remembered the look of surprise on her face when he pulled back the bowstring and the arrow flew through her heart.

"Now, see what you made me do." He'd knelt to arrange

her in the snow and place the wedding veil on her head. "This hurts me more than it hurts you."

She was lying there so peaceful. "What did you think would happen out here? That I brought you all this way for a stupid wilderness wedding?"

He bent down to kiss her. She was perfect, really, with the ice crystals already forming in her eyelashes.

"See what you're missing. See what a gentleman I am. You shouldn't have two-timed me."

His bride had looked beautiful, the veil framing her cold still face, her blood blooming around her like a rose in the snow.

Warmed by sweet memories and the blaze, he reached out to Jennifer, but she vanished as quickly as she had come. He shook himself. The snowstorm must be getting to him.

She was dead. It had been all over the news when they found her body.

He stamped his feet, trying to get the circulation and heat going.

"Where is everybody? Hello! You've got company!"

Was the old fool sleeping? Was that any way to treat a guest? Jonathan stomped off through the cabin. He'd jerk the man out of his bed and teach him some manners. Show him how to respect a frozen traveler whose big heart had landed him in more trouble than he'd expected.

The bedroom was empty. Jonathan helped himself to the blankets on the bed then stormed to the kitchen. He ransacked the place, tossing useless empty dishes and cutlery every which way in his search for something to eat. Nothing but plastic packs of that make-believe food that wasn't even fit for a dog. Who lived like that? Where was the potted meat, the Vienna sausage, the cheese and peanut butter?

And where was the owner? If he was hiding somewhere

with a shotgun, he'd soon discover something more dangerous than a bear had entered his cabin.

Jonathan removed an arrow from his quiver and drew his bow. "HEY!" He pointed his bow and arrow in every direction. "Come out, come out, wherever you are."

There was nothing but dead silence.

"What the devil?"

Jonathan lowered his bow and tried to think straight. There was a cup in the sink. And a long-handled pot. He found the wrappings from one of those freeze-dried so-called meals in the garbage.

Could it possibly be her?

The old biddy had been right. Kate was smarter than she looked. She'd never have survived long enough in the wilderness for him to miss crippling her if she didn't know something about hiking and camping.

Jonathan raced back into the front room. The fire was still going, and the owner was still nowhere in sight.

One of Kate's Facebook comments popped into his mind. A photo of her beside a campfire posing with a man who didn't look like much to Jonathan. *Camping with my dad*, she'd posted. *He cooked, I built the fire. How's that for role reversal?*

He'd thought it was cute at the time, a sweet young thing with her dad. He'd probably gathered the wood and stacked it with just the right amount of kindling then let her strike the match.

The blaze in the fireplace told another story.

Jonathan swung his gaze around the room, searching for signs. There. The sofa pillows stuffed in the window. Only a girl would do that. The old codger who owned the cabin would have taped plastic bags over the hole.

She was here. Everything in his gut told him so. She'd smashed the window, climbed inside then somehow built a fire and found a way to eat that slop.

But where was she?

"KATE!" He bellowed her name then stood still, listening for sounds of shifting or breathing.

Still screaming her name he roared through the cabin once more, kicking open closet doors, ripping off the shower curtain, looking under the bed, overturning furniture. Where could she be?

He kicked through the kitchen door that led to the back porch.

There! He knelt and studied the dusting of snow on the floor. In the corner, over by the woodpile. A small footprint near the wall that hadn't been covered by the mists of snow that still drifted through the screen and around the shutters.

He jerked one of the shutters off the screen. Snow poured through and a blast of wind shoved him backward. He fought for footing and tried to see beyond the porch. Visibility was zero.

There's no way Kate would have tried to escape into the blizzard. Just no way.

Jonathan clawed his way out of the blizzard-force wind and back into the kitchen.

"KATE! YOU CAN'T HIDE FROM ME! I'M GOING TO GET YOU!"

He'd get her if it was the last thing he ever did.

2:00 p.m.

How much longer before he figured out where she was hiding?

Even wrapped in her layers of blankets, Kate shivered. She could hear him down below, rampaging through the cabin, stomping and screaming his threats.

Fear has no place in the mind of an athlete, Coach told her, and she smiled. She was not afraid. She refused to be. She was ready for him.

But she was cold. The tree that had fallen on the front porch had crashed into the attic window. Even though she'd stuffed the holes with some old tee shirts she'd found in the attic, her makeshift patch job was no match for the blizzard. Plus, the lack of insulation let the frigid air creep though like icy fingers.

With stealth movements, Kate took her mylar space blanket from her backpack and threw it on top of her blankets. Her cocoon immediately became warmer. Still, if it weren't for that frothing-at-the-mouth monster downstairs, she'd be sitting in front of the beautiful fire she'd built.

What was he doing now? Adding wood to the fire? Trying to get warm after hunting her down without the benefit of his snowmobile?

Suddenly the pull-down door to the attic rattled.

"I know you're up there, Kate!"

Terror shot through her, and she struggled to tamp it down. She was utterly exhausted, and she ached with the added effort of being still and quiet. She was even trying not to breathe too heavily in case he could hear. If he thought she wasn't there, maybe he'd go away.

He jerked on the string outside the door again, and it creaked.

Kate glanced up at the crossbeams. The rope she'd strung from the beams through the folding stairs on the pull-down door tightened and the knots strained, but it held strong.

"I never give up, Kate. How do you think I captured you? Do you think that detour sign got there all by itself and I just happened along?"

The thought of that depraved mind laying a trap then waiting patiently chilled her soul.

Don't let your opponents make you weak. Echoes of her Coach's voice gave her courage.

The madman was toying with her, trying to beat her with his mind games.

"Hi, girlfriend," he said in a high-pitched voice. "I'm sorry your holidays are going to be so awful... Sad emoji face... I'm driving home Monday and should be there by lunch."

He was Frankie!

Kate felt sick at her stomach. He was quoting her last private Facebook message to her online friend.

"When I get home, I'll see if my parents will buy you a plane ticket so you can join us in Grand Marsais." His girlish imitation and maniacal laughter made her skin crawl.

"You see, Kate, I worked hard to get you. I'm keeping that good fire going down here, and I'll stay as long as it takes. You're mine."

She was fed up with him. And she was more than tired of being hunted.

"Open this door! I know you're there. I saw your tracks." He rattled the door again. "If I have to come up there and drag you back down here, you're going to regret it, Katie."

That was the last straw. Nobody got to call her Katie unless they well and truly loved her.

"So will you," she yelled. "Come on, sucker."

"Kate!"

"Yeah! It's me, you slime ball."

"What did you call me?"

"Sucker! Buffoon! Pond scum!"

He screamed and rattled the door again.

"What have you done to this door?" If he weren't such monster, his screech would be comical.

"I've outsmarted you, creep."

"Open up!"

"Figure it out, stupid."

127

He jerked on the string with a force that almost loosened the knots in the rope securing the attic door.

Kate jumped up and prepared to execute Plan B. The attic was filled with odds and ends of furniture, old clothes, kid's games, a buoy bell and an assortment of other goodies you'd expect in the deep woods cabin of an outdoorsman. Other people's junk had become her arsenal.

It was quiet down below. What was he planning now?

Kate leaned forward listening for the sound of his footsteps. She tracked him as far as the living room, and then she lost him.

What would he do next? She didn't dare let herself panic, and she wasn't going to waste energy standing over the hatch door preparing to execute Plan B.

Picking up her ice ax, she huddled back into her cocoon. She'd positioned it so she had a view of both the opening to the attic and the window.

Those were the only points of access to the attic, and she was prepared to defend both entryways with everything she had.

She pulled her thermos out the backpack and took a long drink. She had to stay hydrated. She had to stay ready to fight.

When she'd first heard Jonathan coming, she'd almost panicked, but then she remembered seeing the string hanging down from the hall ceiling. She'd managed to get all her supplies up the disappearing staircase and into the attic. Thanks to parents who never allowed her to be a helpless hothouse flower, she had roped the folding stairs just above the first hinge, closed the hatch door and then secured the rope to a crossbeam.

While he was raging down below, making as much noise as ten people, she'd quietly explored her new hiding place, confiscated the things she could use, then stuffed the cracks in the broken window and set out to make her hiding place as secure as possible. Her mom and dad would be proud of her.

Where were they? If her car had been found, they'd launch a search with Jefferson from that point. She was absolutely certain of it. Currently, they'd be holed up with Jefferson in their winter tent, waiting out the storm.

Could she hold Jonathan off for the duration of the storm? The earliest reports had said it could last anywhere from three hours to three days.

You have to hold out, Kate. You haven't crossed the finish line.

"I can do it, Coach," she said. "I know I can."

The blow against the attic door shot Kate out of her cocoon. What was that? The second blow was followed by the sound of splintering wood.

She covered her mouth to hold back her scream. There was one important thing Kate had left behind. The ax behind the woodpile.

Jonathan had found it and was chopping his way into the attic.

CHAPTER EIGHTEEN

3:00 p.m.

WHEN KATE SAW the blade of the ax appear briefly in the pull-down door, she was paralyzed by fear, filled by the vision of two dead girls posed in the snow and certain she'd be next. Momentarily helpless, she watched the blade carve away at the barrier between them.

With his next blow, wood chips flew upward, sprinkling her hair and clinging to her clothes. Eventually he would make a hole big enough to climb through.

Move!

Memories of her Coach's voice jolted her out of a trance-like fear. Suddenly Kate felt her blood filling up with ice. She was a glacier, a frozen river, an ocean of deadly icebergs. Newly fortified with the icy resolve of a young woman who would not be posed dead in the snow unless an entire army of villains overpowered her at gunpoint, she mentally prepared herself to fight.

Kate lined up her make-shift weapons. Most she'd found

in the attic, some she'd brought up from the kitchen. Her reliable standbys, the rope and the ice ax, she'd stolen from his own shed.

Somehow it seemed poetic justice to her that she could use a weapon against him that she'd found in the same place where he kept souvenirs of the girls he'd so carelessly slain. As she moved into fighting position, mentally ticking off the order in which she'd use her weapons, she whispered, "This will be for you, Jennifer and Linda."

To Jonathan, she screamed, "Today is not my day to die!"

"Did you think you could keep me out, Kate?"

"I know I can, you lunatic."

"What's a little bitty thing like you going to do to a big man like me?" His unhinged laughter was made even worse by the sound of the ax blade carving away at the portable staircase.

"Let me count the ways. First, the minute you show your ugly face, I might chop off your head." She waited for his response, but all she got was a renewed frenzy of hacking away the entrance to her hideaway.

"But that would be too easy," she added. "I think I'll torture you first. Like you did those other two girls."

There was dead silence, no chopping, no angry response.

"Cat got your tongue?" she yelled. If she could make him mad enough, he might get careless, reckless.

"You're not as smart as you think you are, Kate. I've never had a girlfriend except you."

He started whacking again with renewed fury. Suddenly his ax was through and a hole bloomed across the trap door. He was dangerously close to making an opening big enough to crawl through.

Kate forced down her panic. Icebergs had no fear. They could not be moved. And neither could she.

You've got this, Kate. Her coach's voice echoed through her mind, and cold determination poured through her.

"Dream on, stupid. I'm not your girlfriend. I'm your worst nightmare!"

One more swing with the ax, and he took down the section of pull-down staircase she'd tied to a beam. The rope snapped, pieces of the staircase flew in every direction and the hole widened so that it looked like the Grand Canyon.

The only good news was that he could no longer use the stairs. Kate heard footsteps followed by scraping and dragging sounds. He was bringing something into hall to use for climbing. She didn't dare lean over the hole to look. He might still have his bow, and he might just plant an arrow in the center of her forehead.

"Come on, sucker." Goading might force him to show his hand. "Give it your best shot."

"I'll show you who's boss," he screamed.

Suddenly he grabbed the edge of the opening to the attic, and Kate felt the adrenalin rush of fight or flight. When his head and shoulders popped into view, she shoved the antique trunk with all her might. It hit him smack in the face, and he screamed all the way to the floor.

His body hit with thud, followed by sounds of the trunk banging along the floor.

"Bingo!" she yelled. "Now who's the boss?"

It was quiet down there. She didn't dare peer over the edge. Instead she moved backward so she could get a long-angle view of the hallway. She saw part of the old fashioned steamer trunk she'd used to send him sprawling, an overturned table he'd used to climb on, and a small section of Jonathan's legs, spread out like a cadaver on a slab at the morgue.

Had she killed him? Or was he only knocked out?

Kate went very still, listening. There was nothing but

dead silence below and the screaming storm outside. Holly assaulted the cabin with the ferocity of a pride of lions trying to bring down their prey.

There was no escaping through the window into that blizzard.

Her longing for the fire she'd built downstairs was almost visceral. She could feel the heat against her face, feel the warmth seeping through her skin and spreading through her body. If only she could go downstairs and wait out the rest of the storm in front of the fire, she might be able to put the horrors of the last two days behind her.

She glanced at the rope she'd tied to a crossbeam. He'd whacked off a small portion, but there was still enough she could use to rappel into the hallway.

But what if Jonathan was playing 'possum down there? What if she'd only temporarily addled him and he was waiting for her to walk past so he could grab her? She had every confidence she could get the best of him in a game of wits, but she'd be no match for his size and strength. She'd had plenty of survival and endurance training, but none in hand to hand combat.

They'd offered some defensive courses for women at the University of Minnesota. If she got out—when she got out—she was going to enroll as soon as the new semester started.

Resigning herself to the frigid temperature in the attic, she settled into her cocoon and prepared to wait out the storm or continue her battle with the killer. Whichever came first.

3:45 p.m.

Jonathan came to gradually, his surroundings coming alive in bits and pieces. The floor, hardwood, but missing the scent of lemon oil Betty used on the mop. The walls, stark slabs of wood without the cabbage rose wallpaper Jonathan hated and his mother loved. The ceiling, a jagged hole ripped into it...

He bolted upright and pain shot through his head. His ax had skittered down the hall and an old trunk lay on its side three feet from where he had fallen. His sneaky, conniving bride-to-be had almost killed him. The worst part was she'd done it with nothing more than a trunk.

"KATE! You won't get away with this!"

"I just did, idiot!"

If they were back home and she was leading him a merry chase around the bedroom, he'd admire her spunk. But she'd wrecked his snowmobile, nearly killed him with falling trees, caused him to freeze almost to death and put a knot on his head the size of a baseball.

"You'll pay for this."

"So will you, Mr. Wrong About Everything."

Her laughter was positively wicked. Why hadn't he checked that out before he caught her? If he'd ever heard her laugh, he'd have sent her on her way with a patched tire then groomed another girl.

"What else are you going to do? Throw old clothes at my head?" He was so mad he could hardly see straight. Or maybe the smack-down with the trunk had addled him. "Pelt me with mothballs?"

Kate went quiet up there. That was even worse than her diabolical laughter and her unexpected defensive tactics. Her silence was malevolent. Obviously she was plotting against him. He could almost feel her thoughts reaching through the hole to grab him by the throat.

What else could there be in the attic? Maybe some old furniture, but most of it would be too heavy for her to lift. And a chair small enough for her to toss wouldn't deter him.

Even if there was a second trunk up there, she'd better

take another look at her enemy. He wasn't the kind of man who would sit still for his obituary to read *killed by a flying trunk*

Still, he went through the house looking for a gun. Let her see how she liked looking down the business end of a barrel.

His search turned up no guns, not even a fishing pole. What kind of outdoorsman lived in this rat hole of a cabin? Jonathan stomped into the kitchen and pawed through the cabinets. On the bottom shelf next to the stove he found an old metal sieve, the old-fashioned kind with curved legs you could put on a countertop.

It was the perfect size for his head. By stuffing two kitchen towels underneath, he could add a layer of protection against Kate's next blow.

Wearing the sieve like a helmet, he caught a glimpse of himself in a mirror hanging above the sink. His nose was swollen twice its normal size, his face was raw from being nearly frozen and bleeding from the gash Kate had made in his cheek with the trunk. He looked nothing like the dashing, handsome bridegroom he'd intended to be. More like a creature from a horror show.

And he was going to extract his full measure of revenge.

Back in the hall, he set the table upright and hefted himself up. He craned his neck upward, trying to pinpoint her location. Where was she?

"I didn't want to do it this way, Kate."

"I'm sure you didn't, you coward. You wanted an easy target."

Her voice was coming from his left. He angled his head that way, but she had scooted too far back from the edge for him to see.

"You'd better watch that mouth, young lady. Who do you think you're talking to?"

"The man who shot two innocent girls in the heart with an arrow."

The clever girl had moved to the right. How did she have any energy after being chased in snow all day? She ought to be weak and dehydrated, huddled up without a single ounce of fight left in her.

The others hadn't been as strong as this one. Jennifer had put up a fight, probably because of the baby. But Linda had been so scared she'd wet all over herself and done nothing but whimper.

"But what else would I expect from a coward who mistreats his own sweet mother?" she added. Her taunt felt like molten lava in his veins. He boiled with rage. "That's what you are, isn't it? A coward. A great, big whiny coward."

He leaped upward to catch the edge of the attic floor, and she pounced, shrieking like a banshee. He tried to see what she had in her hand, but it all happened too fast. His fingers slipped and he landed back on the table in a crouch. Pain shot through his bruised leg, and he had to hunker there a moment to recover.

He'd have to outsmart Kate. The trick was to stop rising to her bait, tell her something that would throw her off-balance.

"You think Betty's sweet?" he yelled.

"She was good to me."

"She sent me out here to kill you." That shut her up. He felt a moment of supreme satisfaction, extreme superiority. "I told her the storm would get you, but that didn't satisfy the old biddy. She likes blood."

Let's see how she likes that!

Kate was quiet for so long he wondered if she'd passed out from shock. Pretty little privileged girls like her couldn't fathom how a mother could also be a monster.

"You're lying," she said, finally, but she didn't sound very

137

convinced. More like a bewildered little girl. "Betty's a nice woman."

"Why do you think she kept you locked in?"

"So you wouldn't get to me." She didn't sound so cocky anymore. He congratulated himself on finding this new weapon. It was going to be almost too easy to break her.

"She was jealous of you. She was jealous of them all. Betty will never allow another woman to live in that house."

Kate was quiet up there. Where was all her bravado now? Where was that feisty girl who had run all day through a snowy wilderness and still had enough energy to shove a trunk in his face? He was gleeful at how quickly he'd broken her.

Suddenly, Jonathan was struck by a brilliant plan. It was different from what he'd intended, but wasn't that the mark of genius? To be able to shift strategy when an opening to victory presented itself?

"If you'll come down here and be nice to me, I'll let you live, Kate."

Her continued silence made him nervous. Had he taken it too far? Had he broken her completely the way he had the second girl? That would be too bad. Kate had far more potential than Linda. She'd been a mouse, a nuisance, as expendable as a used bar of soap.

Kate wasn't like that. She had brains, class. She was the kind of woman you'd be proud to call your wife.

What if she could be his, after all?

"We'll sit in front of the fire till the storm blows over, and then we'll go somewhere else to live. Just the two of us."

Why wasn't she saying anything? She wasn't even moving around. Was she thinking it over? Weighing her options?

"We could hunt and fish and live like royalty, just me and you." The vision became so real he could see the two of them deep in the wilderness where nobody would ever travel, living off the land and having babies. "You're smart, Kate. You could home school the kids."

She was still so quiet up there he could picture her mulling it over, maybe dreaming about their little cottage and their first child. A boy. Big and handsome and strong. Just like him. Kate had proved to be a sturdy girl, the kind who would spit out boys as fast as he could make them. After three, he might go for a girl.

Let Betty try to spoil things for him, then. She wouldn't have a clue where they were. She wouldn't have any idea that she had three grandsons with a granddaughter on the way.

With such a picture-perfect family, Jonathan might even try to locate his daddy. In the one photo he had, Harvey looked like a man who would get a kick out of being a grandfather. Maybe they could have Christmas together, surrounded by Jonathan's kids, a holiday both of them would always remember.

Suddenly Kate stomped on the attic floor.

"Hey, down there, Dumbo. Are you listening? I wouldn't have a child with you if you were the last man on earth!"

Fury propelled him off the table and into the front room. Let her stay up there in the cold. Let her wonder what he was up to. He'd make her so tense with worry that the next time he went over the edge and into the attic, she'd never know what hit her.

He had plenty of time. The monster storm was living up to its name. It wasn't likely to be done with Minnesota anytime soon.

And he for sure wasn't done with Kate Carter. By the time he was finished with her, she'd be begging him to put an arrow through her heart.

Jonathan sank onto the sofa and stretched his legs toward the fire. It felt so good he didn't even bother to take the sieve off his head. Come to think of it, he could call it a crown.

After all, he was king of this forsaken cabin. He could sit here and wait for the cover of dark to drag Kate out of that attic.

What would the old biddy think if she saw him now, living like a king while Kate hunkered down in the cold? She might change her tune about who was the dummy of the house and who was the boss.

He pulled out his phone to snap a selfie and send it to Betty, but his phone had gone dead. Last night he'd been so excited to have Kate in the house he'd forgotten to charge it. Probably couldn't get any service out this far anyway. That last call he'd made to Betty was about the limits of service this deep in the wilderness.

It served the old biddy right. Let her sit up there in that big old house and worry about him for a change. It was a whole lot better than him worrying about her, what evil thought she had, what horrible insult she'd hurl his way next, what outrageous thing she would do and say in order to ruin his life.

CHAPTER NINETEEN

5:00 p.m.

BETTY WAS FREEZING to death and furious at everybody she knew. Her power had been off for four hours and that stupid son of hers had forgotten to get fuel for the backup generator. If he ever got home, she was going to make him wish he was dead.

What was taking him so long? He'd caught up with the girl hours ago. Betty didn't care how smart Kate was. It shouldn't have taken this long for Jonathan to kill her.

She watched as the last log burned in two, then wrapped herself in another blanket and went into the kitchen to find something to eat. As it turned out, all she found was some stale bread and peanut butter with jelly.

She'd meant to cook a pot roast with all the trimmings plus a meatloaf to have for the storm, but, oh no. Thanks to that foolish son of hers, her house had turned into Grand Central Station. She hadn't done a thing all day except stand in her front door and fend off foolish questions.

She hoped Maggie Carter was out there in the wilderness buried under an avalanche. It would serve her right for ruining Betty's day.

And that stupid cop need not think he was going to come back nosing around here with a warrant. Betty would shoot him on the spot. She'd use him for fertilizer for her spring garden. If spring ever came. At the rate winter was going, it looked like she was in for another few months of misery.

Betty made herself a sandwich then stood at the kitchen window, eating and peering into the darkness. She hated winter. The horrible weather and the stupid early sunsets. Though who had seen the sun since Holly went on a rampage?

The blizzard was driving her crazy. Shutters banged against the walls and the howling wind tore under and around the house. It was like some crazy giant trying to lift her home off the foundation and rip it to shreds.

Well, let it. She'd move to Florida. Get herself a little cottage on the beach. Without Jonathan.

He was grown now and she wouldn't live forever. Maybe it was time to let him go. Maybe it was time for him to start taking care of himself.

Still, in spite of his many mistakes and the lonely life she'd had devoting all her time to him, she hated the idea that he was out there in the midst of the storm. She didn't want to lose her only child. Thankfully he knew the wilderness well, and he had sense enough to find shelter.

She chased her sandwich with a glass of water. She'd meant to make a pot of coffee, something to warm her up during the storm. But, of course, she hadn't counted on having to think of everything around here, including getting fuel for the generator.

The wind outside her window screeched like a thousand demons. That silly weatherman, Stan, had predicted wind gusts of seventy-five miles an hour. To Betty, it sounded more like a hundred and ten. It sounded like the end of time.

She turned to hurry back to her fire.

Suddenly, the wall ripped off and the gale lifted Betty across a kitchen turned to chaos. She slammed onto her back while shards of glass pelted her. Her furniture flew around her like animation in a Walt Disney movie. The teapot bounced off her head and an upended china cabinet made a hard landing on her hips.

She screamed with pain and couldn't seem to stop. She was pinned to the floor. Every bone in her body felt crushed and broken. Her hips were twisted sideways and the useless sticks that were once her legs didn't seem attached to the rest of her. Even her hands and lower arms were mangled underneath the china cabinet.

"Help!" she cried. "Somebody help me!"

The wind snatched her cries into the maelstrom. The dishes that had been sitting quietly in the sink turned into airborne missiles while her kitchen towels pelted her head like angry demons. A large tea towel featuring a wilderness scene attached itself to her face and wouldn't let go.

She was going to smother to death. If the flying crockery and cutlery didn't kill her first. Panicked, she fought for breath. Her vision was going dim. She was going to die because of a tea towel.

"Help me," she whimpered.

But nobody was there to hear except Holly. The storm took pity on her and lifted the towel off her face. Betty gasped for breath--only to find herself sucking in snow that was now pouring into her house where the wall used to be.

"No, no, no, no, no...."

The snow flew in with a vengeance, first covering Betty with a light dusting, the way she used to sprinkle powered sugar on top of her pound cakes, then piling it on like

Jonathan had when he was five years old and tried to bury his mother in sand.

They'd driven all the way to Biloxi to meet a man Betty had discovered at an online dating site. A year after her husband Harvey had vanished. Back when she was gorgeous and golden and filled with hope.

When had hope died? When she'd found out her online suitor had a wife and six kids and was an alcoholic, as well? When she'd discovered that there was something a little off about Jonathan? When she understood she'd married a spineless, heartless man who would bring her nothing but misery? When she'd realized she was never going to have a charmed life? She was going to be stuck in these Minnesota woods forever with a son who didn't appreciate her.

She blew snow out of her mouth and tried to blink it out of her eyes. For a while, she'd thought she would be buried alive under the snow. But the wind had shifted directions and the snow was now swirling off into the woods.

Fortunately she would not be dying of asphyxiation.

Unfortunately, nothing could stop the cold. No amount of wishful thinking would raise the temperature from twenty below. Her teeth chattered and she shivered violently.

It came to Betty with the same certainty she'd felt when she sent Jonathan out to kill the girls. She was going to freeze to death.

She was so cold she could no longer feel her own skin. She was nothing more than a beating heart encased in an icicle.

Is this what Linda had felt?

Jonathan had killed the first one—Jennifer--quickly. Betty didn't know why. Maybe because of the baby. Maybe because he'd once had some crazy idea that the two of them might make a go of it. In spite of the way his warped brain worked, he'd somehow developed real feelings for her.

But the second one was nothing more than a scared little

mouse. Betty had sent him out to kill her with no more thought than if she'd told Jonathan to set mousetraps in the attic. She'd even reminded him to get back in time for supper.

He'd come back in time, and they'd had a good laugh over their roast beef and gravy when he told how he'd toyed with the girl.

"She was running around naked in the snow, whimpering and peeing herself," he'd said. "I'd let her get ahead of me, just enough to make her think she could get away, and then I'd tackle her and bring her down for a little fun and games. Finally she turned blue all over and was shivering so hard it wasn't fun anymore, so I sat down and entertained myself watching her run in circles till she couldn't run any more."

"How long did it take her to freeze to death?" she'd asked.

"I didn't wait to find out. You know me. I've got a generous heart. I put her out of her misery before she froze to death."

Now Betty was shaking so hard the china cabinet on top of her swayed. But even if her rigors shook it off, she wouldn't be able to move. With all those broken bones, she might not even be able to crawl.

She started crying, but her tears froze in her eyelashes. She wished she knew how long she'd have to wait before she froze. Would she pass out first? She tried to shut out the terrifying thoughts. But nothing could keep them at bay.

Maybe if she tried to stay conscious, Jonathan would get home in time to rescue her. She focused on the dim light coming from the room beyond. Was it coming from the candles she'd lit or was the fire still going? She'd heard of stranger things, hurricanes in the Deep South that tore out a wall, lifted a piano through the hole and left a half-empty can of Coca Cola sitting on the coffee table, undisturbed.

The dim firelight showed her kitchen in shadows...and in shambles. Nothing stirred now, not even the tea towels.

But wait. What was that?

Betty peered through her frozen lashes toward a moving shadow in the far corner of her kitchen. As it stalked closer, she could see the outline of a ghost cat.

It couldn't possibly be.

Was she hallucinating?

Had Linda hallucinated before she died? Had Jennifer?

Would Kate? Would her life flash before her eyes?

With Betty's past running a Technicolor horror show through her mind, the ghosts gathered to hover around her, shroud-like, beckoning with icy fingers while her kitchen dissolved into a bitter, white perdition.

Suddenly a piercing scream split the silence. Betty watched with growing horror as the shadows closed in. First the dead girls, then her husband and finally the cougar, lean and fierce and hungry.

GRAND MARSAIS 9 NEWS

"Holly has been battering Grand Marsais and the surrounding area since one o'clock this afternoon, and she shows no signs of stopping."

As he faced the cameras, Stanley's stomach rolled. He'd thought the hot dogs would settle it down after all those doughnuts, but they had only made his indigestion worse. If this kept up, he was going to embarrass himself on the air.

He hastened through the weather report, pointing out that the blizzard was stalled over Grand Marsais and would last through the night.

"She should show signs of weakening by midnight, and by early morning she is poised to move out, gather force and turn her deadly eye on Cedar Rapids, Iowa." He moved his pointer across the map and finished his spiel just in time to be off-camera when he burped.

Jean had been after him to see the doctor. Maybe she was right.

She hadn't called in the last two hours, and that was a relief. Maybe she was finally over worrying about her parents missing Christmas in Minnesota. Maybe she'd taken a nice long bath and was settled into her easy chair with a good book. Jean loved reading.

He was about to call and check on her when his cell phone rang. It was his wife.

"Jean? Are you okay?"

"I am not!"

"What's wrong, hon? Two hours ago you said the backup generator's working and everything was fine."

"It is NOT fine, Stanley. I'm having a baby."

"I know. And it's wonderful. Just think, in two weeks we'll be parents."

He put as much enthusiasm in his voice as he could muster, but he didn't know if it was enough to fool Jean. The pregnancy was unplanned, and he hadn't been too thrilled when she'd first announced it. It was only in the last few weeks that he'd begun to see himself as having any potential at all for fatherhood.

"The baby is coming now!"

"What? That's not possible."

"Tell it to the baby." Jean let out a wail that raised the hair on his head.

"What was that?"

"A contraction."

The baby couldn't possibly come while he was stuck at the TV station in the middle of a blizzard. He tried to remember everything he'd read about babies and giving birth in the last two months, but he was drawing a great big blank.

"What's the name of that thing that happens when you're not really in labor but you think you are? Something that starts with a B."

"Braxton Hicks contractions, Stanley." His wife was speaking through gritted teeth. Not a good sign.

"Yeah. That's it. It's bound to be Braxton Hicks. Just lie down and relax, Jean. That's what the book says."

"You think so?" It was impossible to miss her full-out sarcasm.

"Yeah, yeah. It'll be all right now. Anyhow, even if it is real labor, that goes on for hours, and I'll be home by morning... Jean, are you crying?... Jean...did you hear me?"

She'd already hung up.

Stan stood helpless and shook his fist at the storm battering the TV station.

CHAPTER TWENTY

9:30 p.m.

JOE SHIFTED IN HIS SLEEP, restless, not unusual for him since 9-11.

He hadn't wanted to take the first sleep shift, but Maggie insisted. She'd grabbed a catnap in the car, she argued. If he didn't get some rest, he'd be of no use to her when the storm lifted and she could take Jefferson out again.

Maggie leaned against her backpack and watched her husband toss in the small confines of the tent. Was he having nightmares about the exploding towers again? Was he dreaming about Kate, lost in the snowstorm? Was he thinking about their babies, lost because of Maggie's stubbornness?

Usually she let him shift away, always moving toward isolation on the other side of the bed. This time, she reached out and put a hand on his shoulder. He stopped tossing a moment, and then as naturally as he had in the early days of their marriage, he shifted toward his wife, moving close enough so that his head rested in her lap.

"There now," she whispered. She stared at her husband, the way his hair turned golden under the glow from the Candoil lamp, the way it still fell across his forehead, as thick as it had always been.

He was a handsome man, always had been and probably always would be. Joe had the kind of face that aged well. When he was eighty, he would look fifty.

Would she? Would they still be together at eighty?

Suddenly she was crying, from sorrow, from fear, but also from a deep well of regret. How many times through the years had she longed to tell Joe what losing the babies did to her? How many times had she wanted to make her burden of guilt lighter by sharing it with him, explaining how she couldn't ignore a child the age of Kate lost in the wilderness, how she'd taken every precaution, how she'd never believed that a woman as physically fit as she wouldn't be able to breeze through a search and rescue with her babies still snug in her womb?

Maggie glanced from Joe to Jefferson. Her dog was sleeping peacefully, occasionally moving his front legs as he dreamed.

He was the most beautiful of her SAR dogs, the most intelligent. And yet each one had performed perfectly in the field, never missing a scent clue, never leaving the lost unfound.

She wished she had explained to Joe how she'd been certain that the hard work of rescue would fall on Kelly's shoulders. She wished she could go back to that hospital bed and tell Joe how sorry she was that the babies were gone. She wished she could tell him it was all her fault.

She should have been more watchful. She should never have tried to climb a path that was too steep and too narrow, a path riddled with loose stones that would catapult her over the edge and into the ravine.

When this is over, she'd said to him earlier this evening. They would talk about everything after the storm was gone, after they'd found Kate.

I'll be here, he'd said. Only three words, but Maggie wove them into a silver chain of hope and hung them over her heart.

Joe might shy away from controversy and go out of his way to avoid a conversation that could turn confrontational, but he never lied. Not to her and not to Kate.

It was that simple. That miraculous.

She ran her hand softly through his hair. "When this is over, Joe, I'm holding you to that promise."

Jefferson made a muffled mock-bark in his sleep, and Joe shifted so that his right arm wrapped around Maggie.

Could they make their marriage work again? After all these years? It wouldn't be easy, and it would require change. On both their parts.

While Maggie's personal storm raged, the blizzard-force winds outside snapped the tops off entire stands of trees and wreaked havoc on the loose snow that had been piling up on the ridge behind the abandoned trading post. Working under cover of dark, Holly readied her assault with the carelessness of Nature turning deadly.

"Please," Maggie whispered, unaware. "Please."

It was both plea and prayer--for Joe, for Kate, for herself, and most of all for the brave SAR dog who was key to finding their missing daughter.

The loose snow picked up speed as it roared down the bluff. Jefferson was the first to hear. When he sat up and barked, Maggie went instantly alert.

"Oh, no!" She shook her husband. "Joe! Avalanche!"

It slammed into the back of the trading post with a force that shot the back door open and sent snow roaring into the storage room.

Joe grabbed Maggie's hand and pulled her from the tent with Jefferson following.

As they raced toward the front, he yelled, "Did you hear it, Mags?"

She instantly knew everything his question entailed. A slab avalanche, the most deadly of them all, announced itself with a thunderous *whumping* sound that was unmistakable.

"No, I didn't."

"You're sure?"

"Positive!"

They were almost at the front door when the roof groaned. It started collapsing at the back, and Maggie watched in horror as it folded inward.

Please God, she prayed. *Let me be right.*

With a sluff avalanche, loose snow piling down from the bluff might bury part of the general store.

If Maggie was wrong, if she had failed to hear the warning sound and this was a slab avalanche, they would be buried alive before they could get out of its path.

9:30 p.m.

Jonathan woke with a start. He was furious to discover he'd fallen asleep and his fire was almost out.

He raced onto the back porch and grabbed more wood, then stoked the fire till it was roaring hot. The glow lit the front room and made a bright path into the hallway.

What was Kate doing? Had she sneaked past him while he dozed? Had she found herself some other hidey hole where she could fight him off?

He stalked back into the hallway and climbed onto the table. The effort cost him, and he groaned with pain. His leg was worse and his head felt as if it had been run over by a Mack truck instead of an attic trunk.

"Kate, I'm coming for you!"

"Come ahead, sucker. See what you get."

Her reply enraged him. Why was she sounding so alert and feisty when he could barely move?

"If you'd get smart, you could be down here cuddled up with me by the fire instead of freezing your pretty buns off in that cold attic."

"Dream on, monster."

"This is your last chance, Kate."

"Yours, too, Dumbo."

"You'll be sorry."

"Take your best shot and we'll see who's sorry."

Jonathan adjusted his make-shift helmet. Just let her shove a spindly chair at his head. He was ready for her. Matter of fact, he was more than ready. When he got into the attic, he'd have her stripped naked and on her back before she could say *pretty please*. When he was finished with her, she'd be begging him to take her off to a cabin in the woods. She'd be pleading with him to let her be his wife and skin his rabbits and fry his fish and have his babies.

But he was going to play it smart this time.

He got very still and quiet so she'd wonder what he was up to. He waited until he could almost hear how her heart beat faster, how fear crept in and she went all girly and uncertain.

Finally he blew out a breath and made one clean leap toward the opening in the attic. His hands connected solidly. No way could a trunk knock him down now. His arm muscles strained as he hefted himself upward.

He could see her now, silhouetted by the glow filtering into the hall from the fire. She was standing there waiting for him. He could already taste her skin.

Even in the faint light she was beautiful. More beautiful than he remembered.

She moved toward him, and he smiled. She was as good as his now.

Chase over. Game finished.

Her pale hair swayed as she leaned down. Her light blue eyes glowed as she reached out to give him a hand.

She was sexy. So sexy.

And she wanted him. Jonathan Westberg. King of the cabin.

Suddenly she moved and pain shot through his right hand. His blood spurted upward. Too surprised to even scream, he glanced down at his hand. A screwdriver went all the way through his palm and into the wood below.

"What did you do?" he screamed. She'd nailed him to the attic floor.

"That was for Jennifer."

She came at him again, right arm extended. Suddenly his eyes caught fire and his whole face burned.

"That was for Linda."

He couldn't breathe, couldn't see. He hung there, a speared marlin, helpless.

He knew that smell. She'd used wasp and hornet spray on him. He was going to die from the poison. He was going to be blinded for life. His skin was going to peel off and he was going to be scarred beyond recognition.

Screeching with rage, he tore the screwdriver out of his hand and toppled from the attic. His back hit the table with a loud crack then he bounced and landed on the floor.

He lay there stunned, his breath coming in gasps. He didn't know what part of his body hurt the most. It took him a full five minutes just to recover his breath. Another five for him to determine that his leg wasn't broken and he could still use the fingers on his wounded hand.

"You're going to pay for this, Kate."

"I doubt it."

"I'm coming up to there to get you and you'll find out what fear really is."

"Haven't you had enough, Dumbo?"

"I'm just getting warmed up. You haven't seen anything yet."

"Neither have you."

He hobbled toward the kitchen and her taunting voice followed him.

"Where are you going, coward?"

Just wait till he was done with her. Long before she took her last breath, she'd think she had died and gone to Hell.

He stumbled in the direction of the kitchen. He could see nothing but shapes, and he was losing blood. It spurted from the wound, rolled down his fingers, dripped onto the floor.

Suddenly the doorframe rose up to meet him. He slammed into it so hard he saw stars.

Kate would pay for that.

He corrected his path and held his good hand in front of him, trying to feel his way. At last, the kitchen. He felt the smooth surface of the stainless steel refrigerator.

He groped his way across to the sink on the opposite wall and turned on the faucets. Nothing came out. Not a drop of water.

Howling with rage, he felt along the top of the cabinet for the tea towels he'd flung about earlier.

There. Something soft.

He wrapped a dish towel around his right hand to stop the bleeding then scrambled around for another to scrub at his face.

Water. He had to have water.

He burst through the kitchen door onto the porch. Where he'd jerked off the shutter earlier, snow had blown through the screen and formed a deep pile. He threw himself down, face first, howling at the cool relief. He licked at the snow, wallowed his face in it, exulted in it.

Who did Kate think he was? A wimp? Somebody she could stop with insect spray?

If he didn't hurt all over, he'd laugh. Had he cracked a rib on the last fall? Every breath he took was painful.

He was going to get her. And he had to do it before the storm ended and that insane Carter woman hunted him down. He'd seen documentaries on how those stupid SAR teams worked. She would send that dog ahead, and he'd be the first one to find Jonathan.

He had a plan for that, too. He'd put an arrow right through the beast's heart. Let that stupid Carter woman see how she liked that.

He lay there plotting until his nose got so cold he could barely feel it. When he rose from his freezing facial, he felt reborn, capable of anything. Especially taking down a girl who had just played her last card.

He had a killing plan. And this time, it was foolproof.

CHAPTER TWENTY-ONE

10:00 p.m.

THE ROOF of the trading post was collapsing from the back, the weight of the avalanche too much for the old timbers to bear. The rumble and roar of falling timbers and shingles, crushed shelves and splintered walls, magnified inside the building.

Joe stood at the front door clutching his wife. Jefferson stood beside her, fully alert. What was he hearing that they didn't?

Outside, the blizzard still lashed the wilderness with such fury it was impossible to see your hand in front of your face. If Joe ushered his family into a blizzard whiteout, it was likely that none of them would survive. But if he kept standing at the door, it was equally likely they'd all be buried under snow.

Had Maggie been right about what she heard? That it was not the deadly slab avalanche? She was smart, capable. But she was also exhausted and worried.

The rumble came closer, bringing down the store foot by foot. Still, the avalanche had not yet reached the front room.

Keep going or stay? He couldn't wait much longer to make a decision.

Don't let it be the wrong one. Please, God, not this time.

"Joe." Maggie tugged his sleeve. "Jefferson has relaxed."

He glanced at the retriever, barely visible now in the faint glow of the Candoil lamp coming from their tent. Maggie's elegant SAR dog was leaning into her legs, licking her hand.

"It's going to be okay, Mags."

"Yes." She stood on tiptoe and kissed the side of Joe's cheek. "Jefferson is never wrong."

"Wish I could say the same for myself."

"You're too hard on yourself, Joe."

The roaring of moving snow subsided as quickly as it had started. A last hanging timber hit the pile of debris at the back of the store and everything became quiet. The door at the back of the front room was still standing. The pocket rocket burner he'd left on the floor was still there. Their tent remained untouched. Except for a sprinkling of snow that had catapulted through the door during the sluff avalanche, the front room in the trading post looked exactly as it had when they'd set up camp.

Joe felt the hard shiver that ran through his wife. "Let's get inside the tent," he said. "You need to rest."

"So do you."

"I've had my turn. You've got to be sharp so we can find Kate."

Thankfully, she didn't argue. Once they were back inside the close confines of the tent, settled into sleeping bags in the warm glow of the Candoil lamp, Maggie fell asleep quickly.

Joe studied the curve of her long lashes, the way her black hair lay in ringlets against her fine cheekbones, the way she slept with her hands folded and tucked under one cheek, like a child at prayer.

She looked peaceful in sleep. Was it true? Had she disappeared into a dream world where their daughter was asleep in her own bed and Maggie had never found two dead girls in the snow? Where there had never been a psychopath chasing Kate through a blizzard in the wilderness?

His wife sighed, a soft sound that made her smile in her sleep.

What was that all about? Was Joe in her dreams? Were they young again and so much in love she'd couldn't imagine life without him?

"I'm going to make this work, Mags," he said, softly so as not wake her. "As soon as we find Kate, I'm going to make us good together again. I promise."

The blizzard howled around the trading post and the darkness seemed never-ending. He said a prayer for his daughter, somewhere out there in the middle of a nightmare.

Then he said a prayer that he could keep his promise.

11:00 p.m.

It was quiet downstairs. Too quiet.

Kate huddled in her cocoon in the cold dark attic, fighting her growing worry and her need for sleep. Storms still raged around her, inside the cabin and out. And both of them were capable of killing.

How long before the maniac would come after her again? How long would she remain strong and alert enough to keep him out of the attic?

She drank some of her water and ate a piece of beef jerky. Temporarily revived, she shone her small flashlight around her hiding place. Had she done enough to prepare for his next assault?

Don't second guess yourself.

This time she had no doubt that Coach was with her only in her mind. This time she didn't even have to hear the sound of her own voice to believe she was still capable of fighting off Jonathan.

Kate stretched out and consciously relaxed, starting with her toes and moving upward. Her eyes grew heavy…

The clanging of a buoy bell shot her out of sleep. She sat a moment, disoriented. And cold. She was so cold.

The buoy bell started clanging again, and it all came flooding back. Her flight through the wilderness and into the attic. Her desperate measures to protect her hideaway.

She'd rigged both entrances—a rope to secure the attic door and a buoy bell to alarm her if anyone tried to climb the fallen tree and come through the window.

Jonathan was in the tree, and he was coming after her. He was close, too.

Even as tall as she was, Kate's reach hadn't extended far out the window. Earlier she'd managed to attach the buoy bell, but it was in the topmost branches.

She jumped out of her nest of blankets to grab her ice ax and her penlight. Her heart racing, she crept across the attic and stationed herself on the left side of the window.

When she heard him on the roof, she tightened her grip on the ax. Could she do it? Could she strike hard and fast? She would wound him badly, possibly even kill him. Did she have it in her to take another person's life?

Don't think that way, she told herself. This is life or death. *Focus.*

"I've got this, Coach," she whispered.

Suddenly Jonathan rammed the window and glass flew everywhere.

Wait. Wait.

"Did you think I wouldn't get you?" he yelled. He whacked the window again and splinters of glass rained onto the floor. "There's no escape now, girly. I tore up the stairs."

His maniacal laughter was followed by a large shadow creeping through the window.

Adrenaline pumped through her, and still she waited.

"You're going to be sorry, Kate!"

One of his feet touched the floor, and the small animal spring trap snapped with a satisfying thump.

Bingo.

Howling, Jonathan scrambled through. When his other foot hit the marbles she'd scattered on the floor underneath the window, he went down, sprawling in every direction.

His furious screeches were cut short by a loud thump as his head slammed against the windowsill.

Kate flicked on her light and pinpointed her target. He was on the floor, one foot caught in the trap, knocked out cold. Cold being the operative word. Snow flew through the window as if the blizzard were intent on burying him alive.

Kate held the penlight in her mouth and lifted the ax. One whack. That's all it would take. His carotid artery would open and he'd bleed to death. He'd die a slow, torturous death, just like Jennifer and Linda.

Her mother hadn't talked about finding the dead girls. She never talked about any of her grisly SAR missions.

But there had been plenty of details on the news and all over the internet. Kate and her girlfriends knew them all, talked about the murders in hushed whispers at pajama parties and on lazy Saturday afternoons when they'd gather at the Dog and Suds.

They couldn't stop themselves. They were alive and the girls, who could have been any one of them except for a twist of fate, had been raped and killed in the most brutal way possible. Then they'd been found naked in the snow with wedding veils on their heads. They'd probably been chased down like animals.

The attic suddenly felt surreal. Kate's hands shook and tears streamed down her face.

She was strong. One strike would do it. She'd be safe and the dead girls would be avenged.

All her girlfriends had said they'd kill the murderer if they could.

They'd even discussed the ways. Sally said she'd shoot him without thinking twice. She had a permit to carry, and she regularly practiced at the shooting range. Teresa kept mace in her purse. Not surprising since her dad was a detective. She said she was going to put some brass knuckles in there, too. Once the killer was down, she'd beat him so badly he'd wish he were dead. Teresa was already enrolled in a local self-defense course, and her skills put her at the top of her class.

Now the madman lay at Kate's feet, helpless.

She drew back to strike. Her hands shook. Once she killed him, she could never go back. She could never again look in the mirror and see herself without the stain of brutality on her soul.

Slowly, she lowered the ax. She couldn't do it. Not like this, cold-blooded and calculating.

Maybe in the heat of moment, she could.

She hoped she'd never have to find out.

She lashed the ax to her backpack and searched the attic for something to tie him up. Her rope was there, but she needed it to rappel down to the first floor. Jonathan's table was still under what was left of the attic trap door, but what if she made a misstep trying to jump and land there?

Kate couldn't afford to break her leg, or even twist an ankle. After the storm, she might have to hike back—and she was a very long way from home.

She found some old pants and used the legs to tie Jonathan's wrists and ankles. Then she shoved a ratty wing chair into place and tied him to the legs with the sleeves of a button-down shirt.

She considered removing the spring trap from his foot, but images of the other captive girls popped into her mind. She left the trap on.

Kate quickly gathered her supplies and dropped them though the hole to the floor below. One last look told her Jonathan was still out cold. Already he was covered with a blanket of snow.

How long before that same snow woke him?

"Sleep tight, sucker."

She rappelled down, grabbed her supplies and raced into the front room. The fire was nothing more than a few sputtering embers.

She hurried off for more wood and built it back to a fine roar, then went into the hall to listen. All was quiet in the attic.

Had he come to? Was he lying there plotting, working himself free?

Had the blow to his head killed him? He'd gone down hard. Considering his other falls, it could have been the last straw--a killing blow.

"Don't count on it. Move!"

Her pep talk sent her into the kitchen where she set to work gathering the things she needed for her new line of defense. She had no idea whether any of it would work. But she didn't dare sit in front of the warm fire, helpless and hoping he'd remain in the attic trussed up like a turkey.

Kate grabbed the mop, then lugged it along with her arsenal into the hall. A sound stopped her in her tracks.

She stood perfectly still, listening. Outside, Holly felled trees, moaned around the cabin and rattled the eaves. But this sound was different. Creepy. The kind that raised chill bumps along her arms.

Kate strained to separate the new sound from the storm. Finally she heard it. A thumping in the attic. Then, groans.

She didn't have a minute to lose. The monster was awake, the indestructible madman who refused to give up. The flimsy bonds she'd fashioned with old clothes would never hold him.

Soon, he'd be coming to kill her.

GRAND MARSAIS NEWS 9

The Doppler Radar map behind Stanley had everybody at Channel 9 breathing a sigh of relief. The reflectivity of the snowstorm, evident in the glowing red mass on the map, showed Holly was done with Grand Marsais and moving rapidly out of northern Minnesota.

Hyped on coffee and nerves, Stan the weatherman was proud of the way he maintained his outward cool as he moved his pointer over the path of the storm. He was even proud to be standing on his feet, awake. Being at the station during weather disasters was his job, and he congratulated himself on doing it well.

No, not just well. He'd excelled.

"Holly turned her brutal eye southward this morning at three a.m.," he said, proud of how his hands didn't shake.

Inside, he was a wreck. The last he'd heard from Jean, she was screaming with contractions, the ambulance was trying to get to her and he had to go on the air.

"The monster snowstorm is cutting a straight path over Lake Superior and will graze the western side of Wisconsin before she picks up force and turns her deadly eye here." He let his pointer hover over Iowa.

"Cedar Rapids will be the hardest hit, with sustained winds exceeding forty miles an hour. Gusts topping seventy-five miles an hour have pounded northern Minnesota for the last fourteen hours, and Iowa can expect the same."

He paused to let the statistic sink in. Reports of houses collapsing all over northern Minnesota and people trapped inside had been coming in since last night around seven. Reporters were scurrying around, trying to put statistics together for the morning news. Only three hours from now.

Stan didn't envy their job.

"Grand Marsais will feel the effects of snowstorm Holly for several more days. It's still not safe to be on the roads. The roads on your screen are closed."

The list scrolled on the screen behind him as he talked. "These nurseries, day care centers and businesses are shut down until further notice."

The list was shorter because school kids were out for the Christmas holidays, and public schools had closed days earlier. A real blessing in weather like this. There were always foolish parents who didn't check the news and spun over icy embankments trying to get their kids to school.

"Until we dig our way out of this snowstorm, be safe, be smart. As always, Stan the weatherman is here in Grand Marsais, Channel 9 News, looking out for you!"

He jerked off his microphone and grabbed his handkerchief out of his pocket to swab off his stage makeup.

"Stan!" Larry Goddard, one of the VPs of the station, hurried toward him. "The ambulance got your wife to the hospital, and we've got a wrecker out front to take you there."

"Thanks, Larry. I owe you one."

"No, we owe *you,* Stan. Great weather coverage."

Stan hurried out of the TV station and nearly lost his

footing on the front steps. He caught the railing and held on for dear life. He didn't have time to fall.

When he got into the wrecker, he said, "How fast can you get me to the hospital?"

"Not fast, not in this weather. But I can get you there in one piece."

True to his word, the driver of the wrecker, who turned out to be the father of three and the grandfather of six, delivered Stan to the hospital just in time to wash up, robe up and watch his daughter being born.

"She's beautiful." He leaned down to kiss his wife.

"What would you think if we named her Holly?"

He thought it was the worst idea he'd ever heard. After the storm watch marathon he'd been through, he didn't want to hear that name again as long as he lived. Besides, he and Jean had already decided if they had a girl she'd be called Marianne.

Jean beamed at him. "I just think it would be appropriate, Stan. And so *cute*."

"The name's perfect, hon."

He glanced down at his red-faced daughter. Already, the name was growing on him.

CHAPTER TWENTY-TWO

DECEMBER 23
6:00 a.m.

IT WOULD SOON BE DAYLIGHT, and Joe was already squatted beside the burner making breakfast. He looked up and smiled when Maggie came out of the tent with Jefferson. In the dim light coming from the burner and the Candoil lamp inside the tent, he appeared to be the Joe of old, keeping his own turmoil at bay while trying to shore up her courage. She felt both comforted and filled with renewed promise.

"I've got coffee, Mags."

"Great."

She fed and watered Jefferson while he poured her a cup. Then she sat beside him and held one hand out to the heat coming from the burner.

It was completely dark outside, but the cessation of howling winds and falling trees meant the blizzard was over. Still it was impossible for Maggie to see the terrain she'd be facing when they set out to find Kate. She knew from experi-

171

ence that, post-snowstorm, it would be treacherous. Thirty-foot drifts. Crusts of snow covering deep hidden pockets where you could sink up to your neck or over your head. Shifting slabs underneath the snow, just waiting for some small movement to create a deadly avalanche.

Plus, after nature's massive display of fury, it would be harder to find any of the signs Kate might have left to mark her trail. Though Jefferson was perfectly capable of seeing in the dark and picking up scents impossible to humans, particularly in the early morning hours when those scents lay closer to the ground, she didn't dare take him out post-blizzard before daylight. There was too much risk she and Joe would fail to see one of the many new traps Holly had laid for them.

As Maggie sipped her coffee and mentally prepared herself for the search ahead, she reached into her left pocket to close her hand around Kate's lucky buckeye.

"Do you think she survived the storm, Joe?"

"I'd bet money on it. Kate's one of the smartest and mentally toughest young women I've ever known. She's just like you, Mags."

There'd been a time when Maggie would say, *Flattery will get you everywhere.* When she and Joe would come together as naturally as sunflowers seeking the sun. When their joining would transcend the physical and become the closest thing to spiritual Maggie could imagine—with the exception of rare moments when you allowed yourself to be an innocent child, climbing into the lap of God.

Her sudden need for something beyond the physical realm overwhelmed her. Support. Strength. Hope.

Please.

Her silent, desperate plea was a prayer, a mother's heart yearning for the safety of her child.

She reached for Joe's hand. "Thank you for saying that."

"I mean it. You're a rock star, Mags. And I haven't been the best of fathers. I don't pretend to be."

"Don't say that. There's no yardstick for parenthood."

He squeezed her hand, and the look he sent her was pure, unfathomable gratitude.

"There's one thing I know about our daughter, Mags. We taught her how to survive in the wilderness."

Even in a storm like Holly? Maggie squelched the thought before she could say it aloud. Let Joe have his hope. Hadn't she been reaching for the same thing? Maybe together they could hang on long enough to get through the brutal day that lay ahead.

7:15 a.m.

The three of them stood in front of the trading post, gear stowed in their backpacks, Jefferson in his SAR harness and still on the lead.

Joe assessed the terrain. Fallen trees littered what had once been a parking lot. The avalanche had caved in the entire back of the store, and the bluff behind it had a treacherous snowdrift leading up to it. The scene was daunting, and only an inkling of what lay ahead.

He mentally geared himself for the search while he studied his wife and her SAR dog. Jefferson was straining against his leash, his nose pointing toward the bluff.

Made sense. His daughter would seek the high ground so she could get her bearings.

"I don't want to take him off lead yet and send him into that." Maggie nodded toward the massive piles of snow on the leeward side of the bluff. "Let's head windward."

His wife's sensible call sent a rush of relief through Joe. This morning after breakfast, Maggie had become an emotional mess. Her hands shook as she fastened her backpack, and tears sprang to her eyes when she turned to him.

"I'm not a rock star, Joe. I'm scared to death I'll let Kate down."

"We're in this together, Mags. Why don't I handle Jefferson today and give you a breather? He'll work with me."

That'd she'd even considered the idea showed the depth of her turmoil. Finally she'd assured him that she could do it, she was fine.

Was she all right, or was this another case of Maggie saying fine when she meant exactly the opposite.

Now, Joe studied his wife.

She's going to make it. She's strong.

He turned his attention to the avalanche. As expected, it had moved west to east, sweeping up the loose snow and chunks of ice and pushing it along in front. Though the west side of the bluff wouldn't be the shortest route up, it would be the least hazardous.

While they worked their way west around the bluff, it was obvious Jefferson had caught a scent—and equally obvious he knew what he was doing. As if Maggie had read Joe's mind, she let the big Lab off lead. He loped off, a streak of mahogany against the glaring white of new snow under the first rays of morning light. If you didn't know the life and death nature of his mission, you'd be awestruck by the majesty and beauty of his search.

They didn't catch up with him until they were at the top of the bluff. Maggie moved ahead and disappeared around the corner of a natural wall created by a large boulder.

"In here, Joe," she called.

He found her just inside the small opening of a cave, holding something that glinted gold in her gloved hand. Maggie was too overcome to talk, but her face said everything.

She handed him the object, a thin chain of gold with a heart-shaped disc at its center. His heart squeezing with both fear and hope, he stepped outside to catch the rays of sunlight. The letters KMC were etched there. Kathryn Margaret Carter. His Katie.

He imagined her climbing the bluff while a killer chased her. He pictured her hiding in the cave, waiting for the right moment to run. Kate had a level head. She wouldn't take off running out of fright. She'd consider the problem and find the best solution before she acted.

The anklet had been Joe and Maggie's gift on her eighteenth birthday.

"I'm never taking it off," she'd said.

He remembered the joy in her face, the way her eyes shone with both fierce love and steely determination.

What had been going through his daughter's mind when she parted with this prized piece of jewelry? What quirk of nature had pushed the snow downhill to cover half the trading post and leave the cave open for its discovery? What gift, what unutterable prayer had made it possible for her parents to find yet another sign that Katie had been alive at this spot?

The anklet was proof she'd been clear-headed and determined, two of the biggest factors that would play into whether they found her dead or alive.

Maggie moved out the cave and into the sunrise, blinking at the change of light.

"It has her initials, Mags."

"I knew the minute I picked it up." Maggie shaded her eyes and swiveled around, looking into the distance. Suddenly, she pointed. "Look, Joe. Do you see that?"

In the distance were the lakes, glinting silver in the rising sun. Beyond was a small clearing. And miracles of miracles, what appeared to be a cabin.

Excitement and pride exploded through Joe. "Katie came here to hide, but she also came here to search."

"Yes, she did." Turning to him, her eyes glistening with tears, Maggie leaned briefly against his chest.

Another time, another place, it would have been a moment to savor. But Maggie pulled back to give Jefferson the search command. Then they raced back down the cliff and into the storm-battered wilderness.

Jefferson was slowing now, working crosswind patterns, while Joe and Maggie both strained their eyes into the blinding distance.

There were no further signs from Kate. Had the killer been too close for her to pause and leave a broken branch? Or had her signs been obliterated when Holly roared through, ripping and uprooting trees, slamming them around so they now littered the forest floor like so many matchsticks?

Even now, the wind was still strong enough to create random eddies. Though swirling snow no longer obscured an entire landscape, it played havoc with their ability to see a trail, fresh or otherwise.

Thank God for Jefferson. As he picked up speed, Maggie forged ahead, keeping pace with her dog. Soon she was barely visible, and her Lab was too far ahead to see.

Around him lay a wasteland of blinding white. Joe fought against a creeping sense of discouragement.

Suddenly his wife trotted back. "Have you seen any signs, Joe?"

"No. But we can't make anything of it because of Holly."

"I know. Still..." Maggie went silent and bit her lower lip.

"Mags, Jefferson's still on her trail. We're going to find her."

Neither of them dared say what was on their minds.
Will we find her alive?

CHAPTER TWENTY-THREE

9:00 a.m.

FROM THE DISTANCE, Maggie could see Jefferson circling around what appeared to be a snowmobile.

"Joe!" She raced toward her Lab as she yelled for her husband. "He's got something!"

She squatted beside her dog. "Good boy. Good Jefferson."

Still heaping praise and treats on him, she studied the scene. What was left of the snowmobile lay on its side against a small boulder. Random parts lay scattered around the wrecked snowmobile, half hidden by fresh snow.

Jefferson started to dig, unearthing more machine parts.

As her husband raced toward her, Maggie flashed back to the snowmobile tracks that had converged with her daughter's trail, and to the horrible woman at the farmhouse whose shifty eyes revealed she was lying about her son being inside.

Joe came alongside her and leaned over to catch his breath. It struck Maggie that they were no longer young.

They didn't have forever to make things right between them. If the monster had already caught Kate, she would die thinking her parents hated each other.

Don't go there.

"It's his, Joe." She didn't need proof. Jefferson had alerted here and she felt it in her bones. "I'm glad he wrecked it."

"He'll never catch Kate on foot. She's too fast."

To her right, Jefferson alerted once more then started digging with a fury. Maggie trotted over and squatted beside him.

There. In the hole. A single arrow.

Terror seized her.

Her mind swung wildly back to the frozen girls, each felled by a single arrow in the heart. The sign of an expert marksman. The sign of a depraved murderer. He wanted the world to know he'd killed for love. In case they didn't get the message, he'd arranged wedding veils on his victims' heads. The purest symbol of love, a woman's virginal head-covering, worn on the day she pledges herself to her husband.

She felt the weight of Joe's hand on her shoulder, the utter relief of his solid presence at her side. It wasn't until he knelt beside her and gathered her close that Maggie realized she was crying.

The madman who had wrecked his snowmobile was hunting her daughter with a bow. The unexpected hatred and cold resolve filling her was so shocking, she no longer even knew who she was.

"When Jefferson finds him, I'm going to kill him."

"Shh." Joe pulled her close. "Kate's going to be all right, Maggie. We have to believe that."

Her radio crackled to life, jerking Maggie out of her nightmarish thoughts.

"Maggie?" It was Roger, coming through a thin stream of static. "Are you and Joe all right?"

She shook her head and handed her radio to Joe.

"We made it through the storm," Joe told him. "How about you?"

"We got lucky. Lost some trees, but otherwise we're fine." Roger's voice faded in a brief burst of static, then came through again. "Joe, I'm here at the Westberg house. Our prime suspect is not here."

"He was here." Joe gave his location and described the wreckage, including the arrow.

"If it matches the arrows found in the Olsen and Stephenson girls and we can get prints, we've caught a lucky break. I'll send a forensics team."

"We think the killer's still out here somewhere, chasing Kate. We've got to find her before he does."

"Be careful. He's cagey and he's dangerous. We found the dead girls' licenses in the shed out back."

The thought of her daughter in that house sent a fresh wave of terror through Maggie. "What about that horrible woman?"

"Storm got the entire back wall of her house, Maggie. And Betty Westberg, too. Or what's left of her. Looks like a cougar got to her. We found its tracks and scat in the corner."

Maggie wrapped her arms around herself, shivering, not so much from cold but from the grisly news. The search for Kate had taken a gory turn. She didn't even want to consider what that might mean for her daughter.

She was trying to hold down her breakfast when someone on the other end yelled, "Hey, Johnson!" Male voice. One she didn't recognize. "Over here! Behind the wall!'

"Gotta go," Roger said. "They've found something."

He signed off, and Maggie set off once more with her husband and her dog.

Don't give up, Kate. I'm coming.

10:30 a.m.

The endless vista of glaring white was so disheartening, Maggie felt as if she were on the surface of the moon. In the freezing cold and the surreal setting, she fought to keep her grip on reality.

Where was Jefferson? Where was Kate?

Maggie's head felt like a helium-filled balloon. Was she losing it?

A hand on her arm pulled her back from the brink of a dark mental abyss. It was Joe, offering water.

"We need a break. Call him in."

Within minutes of her call, she saw the flash of her loyal dog's SAR vest. When he trotted to her side, gratitude poured through her, easing out the fear, nosing aside the horror. While Joe watered him, she buried her hands in Jefferson's fur. Clinging to a hundred plus pounds of muscle and pure love, it was impossible to consider revenge, unthinkable to plan pay-back death.

"Are you all right, Mags?"

"Yes," she said, and meant it. She had to be okay. As she re-hydrated herself with water, she filled herself back up with resolve. If she lost courage, she'd lose Kate, too.

Maggie assessed her dog, searching for any signs she should pull him from the search for a longer break. Jefferson stared back at her in the unsettling way that made her think he could read her mind. There was a deep well of kindness in his eyes, total trust and an empathy that felt uncanny.

"Good boy, Jefferson. Good boy." She bent over to hug her dog, as much for herself as for him. Then she straightened up and took command. "Search, Jefferson. Find Kate."

Fifteen minutes later came the Lab's alert. Two arrows in the snow, less than ten feet apart.

Maggie felt as if someone had stuck a cattle prod to her heart. Here, the monster was still alive. Chasing Kate.

She surveyed the area for tracks.

Nothing. Just ground snow rising and falling in the wind, teasing her, leaving her with more questions than answers.

Had the killer lost the arrows in the heat of the chase? Or had they blown free in yesterday's storm and by some freak of nature landed in a spot swept clear by swirling winds?

Even worse, had they landed here after the storm? While he was shooting at her daughter?

"Joe!"

As her husband hurried toward her, Jefferson leaned against her legs, sensing her mood and offering comfort. She hooked up his lead, not out of necessity but from a need to control at least one detail of this heart-wrenching search.

Joe spotted the arrows and immediately sank to his knees. He was so still, he might have been praying or mourning. Or both.

Finally he said, "The arrow's the same as the one at the snowmobile wreckage."

Joe would know. He sold them at Carter's Trading Post, and he made it his business to know his merchandise. The bookshelves in his office at the house and the one at the trading post were lined with biographies of famous fishermen and hunters, trackers and climbers, field guides, histories of outdoor equipment and weapons of every kind, including bows and arrows.

"See this shaft." He pointed, but Maggie had no clue what she was looking at. "It's Forgewood. Bill Sweet of Oregon created this compressed design to strengthen the arrow."

Easier to bring down a six-point buck—or a nineteen-year-old girl you'd lured off to torture and kill.

Had the monster taken Kate by surprise, or had he enticed her in some way? What sick combination of love and hate had driven him to chase her daughter through the wilderness with a bow and arrow?

Maggie thought she'd be sick on the spot.

Joe pointed out the other characteristics that made the arrow distinctive. It had three feathers, and the one leaning to the right was called a cock feather.

All she could do was picture the sort of man cocky enough to believe that her brilliant, educated, talented daughter would ever become his wife. She wanted to scream.

Joe got on his radio to report the details of their location and latest find.

"Looks like this is our man," Roger said. "Great work, you two."

Maggie saw nothing to celebrate. Not one single thing. She felt like taking off her gloves and giving somebody the one-fingered salute. Just about anybody would do.

"Jefferson is the real hero, here," Joe said.

At last, something she could agree with. Still, she wished they'd wind up the conversation. Kate was still out there, and they were wasting precious time.

"No argument from me."

"It looks like he's still alive, Roger. Maybe close. And still after Kate."

"When you find him, don't attempt to handle the situation yourself. You got that, Joe?"

"She's my daughter."

"If he's still got her hostage, he could kill her. We'll send a chopper." Static covered Roger's voice, and Maggie mouthed, *Let's go.*

Joe nodded, and suddenly Roger's voice came through loud and clear. "Joe, these people are extremely dangerous. We've got another body here at the house. Bones in a barrel we found in a closet or pantry of some sort, boarded up at the back of the kitchen. Storm uncovered it."

Horror filled Maggie. "Another girl?" she asked.

"From the size of the bones, looks like an adult male. I'm telling you. When you find the Westberg guy, stay put till we can get a chopper out there."

"Will do," she told him.

Thankfully, Joe signed off before Roger could say anything else.

As Maggie took Jefferson off lead once more and gave him the search command, she told herself she hadn't really made Roger a promise. Nothing that would bind her, make her feel guilty later. More like a vague statement that could be taken either way. Something to give her wiggle room.

When Jefferson found where the monster held Kate captive, she didn't know if she'd have the discipline to wait for backup.

Powered by adrenalin, willpower and a mother's love, Maggie pushed forward through the relentless landscape, trying to keep close pace with her dog. A pale sun pushed through the clouds, increasing the glare.

When she saw the cabin in the distance, she could hardly believe her eyes. Mirage? Wishful thinking?

Jefferson was streaking now, a rich brown blur against the snow. He stopped briefly to alert—another arrow in the snow. Then he was off again, tail waving like a flag.

Maggie was aware of her husband, somewhere behind her, stopping to check the arrow; of her beloved chocolate Lab, moving with purpose; of the cabin, closer now, so close she could see the fallen tree that had taken down half the front porch.

Smoke wafted from the chimney. Someone was in there.

Suddenly Jefferson came to a halt. Maggie's heart stopped beating. Her dog was still standing.

Please, let him keep standing.

She waited, holding her breath.

Jefferson gave one bark. Dogspeak for *found*.

He was not only still standing, but was now making happy circles. *Found alive*.

Her daughter was alive.

CHAPTER TWENTY-FOUR

11:00 a.m.

THE BARK POUNDED through Jonathan's head like a thousand drums. It was a huge sound, deep and forceful, the kind made by big dogs who think they're the king of the hill.

The monster dog had found him. Just wait till Jonathan got his hand on his bow and arrows. He'd put a hole big as a fist right through the stupid dog's head.

And Maggie Carter's, too. He pictured her. Out there in the snow. Gloating. Her belly full of food like that freeze-dried trash he'd found in the kitchen.

His own stomach growled, and self-pity welled up inside. He would do just about anything for a steak. He was starving to death.

And it was all Kate's fault. Stupid girl. He should have killed her right there on the road beside her car. Probably would have if he'd known she could be so much trouble. Definitely would have if he'd known she would turn out to be so selfish.

He deserved a better wife than Kate. A sweet girl who would appreciate his big heart and handsome looks. Of course, it would take a while for his face to get back to normal. But he was the kind of man who could overcome frostbite and hornet spray. Not to mention a few cuts and bruises from the trunk.

Jonathan tried to flex his wounded hand, but it was swollen so big he couldn't even move his fingers. And he didn't want to think about his legs. He needed a doctor.

He needed a change of scene, too. This rat hole of a cabin was getting tiresome. Anywhere would be preferable to a place where a man couldn't even go to the bathroom.

Even jail.

He listened for the dog from Hell to bark again, but it was so quiet out there you'd think he was all alone in here.

Major mistake. The footsteps headed his way belonged to Kate Carter.

She appeared in the hallway, holding a cup.

"Want some hot tea?" She inspected him like he was a bug under a microscope.

He was trussed up like Betty's Christmas turkey. Kate had tied his legs and arms together with rope then bound his mouth with Duct tape. She'd even wrapped the tape around his arms and chest. It would take Houdini to get out.

"No, I guess not." She smiled, then stepped closer, being careful of the slick patches where she'd poured cooking oil on the floor.

She'd even mopped oil all over the opening he'd made in the attic. When he'd finally gotten loose from that silly pair of pants she'd used to tie him up and taken the trap off his foot, he'd slipped through the hole like a greased hog. Broke his bad leg and probably his good leg, too.

That fall had knocked him out, but good.

When he woke up, he saw he'd wet all over himself. She

hadn't even bothered to mop it up. Just trussed him up and gone off to sit by the fire all night while he lay there on the stone-cold floor in his own urine.

She'd even made breakfast this morning and hadn't offered him a bite. She'd just stood in the hall with her heaping plate and said now he knew how those poor captive girls had felt.

Kate was worse than Betty. He was glad her stupid mother and the stupid dog had found him. He needed rescuing from the little witch.

She gave him another wicked smile. "I came to say goodbye."

Good riddance was more like it. He couldn't wait for her to go.

"I'm going home with my parents and Jefferson, and you're going to prison."

Prison would be a welcome relief from her. He couldn't wait for her to get out of his sight.

Unfortunately, his fall had positioned him so he had a clear view of her all the way to the front door.

She walked off like a princess. When she got to the front, she skirted the marbles she'd scattered. The buoy bell she'd hung on the door clanged when she opened it, and Kate walked into the light.

CHAPTER TWENTY-FIVE

11:10 a.m.

WHEN JOE'S daughter walked through the door, he fell to his knees and cried. A castoff snowsuit bagged around her, her gloves were mismatched, her face was raw and peeling and her hair was a tangled mess. He'd never seen a more beautiful sight in his life.

Maggie got to her first. They fell into each other's arms, crying and talking at the same time. Joe gave his wife and daughter their private moment. When Kate told her mother she'd tied up her captor and he was in need of a doctor, Joe's chest swelled with pride.

He and Maggie had done something right. Proof was standing three feet away.

"That's my girl!" Maggie told her. Then his wife moved quickly into finding out what the monster had done to Kate.

"I'm fine, Mom. Don't worry"

When his daughter added that the monster hadn't

touched her, not in that way, Joe felt his entire body unclench. The nightmare was finally over.

Almost.

He made the radio call to Roger that sent an AW180 SAR helicopter into the wilderness. Along with its normal staff of two pilots, a console operator, paramedic rescue diver and attendant, the chopper had an eighteen passenger capability--plenty of room to bring a team of detectives and forensics experts in and airlift Joe's family out. Including the other hero of the day, Jefferson.

Jonathan Westberg left the wilderness on a litter shoved up against the chopper's hospital wall. He was hooked up to IVs and they'd finally given him enough pain medication to knock him out. His silence was a welcome relief from the screaming and ranting and whining he'd done when the paramedic tore the duct tape off his mouth.

Fortunately the hospital wall was at the back and the attendant had closed off the section with a curtain. Though Joe and his family were vividly aware of his presence, at least they didn't have look at him.

Kate seemed perfectly fine riding along in the same chopper with the monster. And why wouldn't she? She'd whipped him at every turn, mentally, emotionally and physically. She'd rendered him helpless, a slobbering wreck of a man.

Joe and Maggie had heard the full story while they waited for the chopper. That Kate was not traumatized and was still strong enough to talk about her ordeal was remarkable. That she had survived it was a miracle.

Joe couldn't have been prouder of his daughter. His Katie would be fine. She had the resiliency of youth and a loving family on her side.

He glanced at his wife. Would they be a loving family going forward?

Though Maggie clung to Kate's hand and smiled at their daughter, she still carried the rigors of the search in her stiff posture. She still carried the trauma in her tight jaw and her eyes. Especially her eyes. The warm spark was missing. And in its place was a deep uncertainty.

Maggie was holding something back, and she was barely holding herself together.

The snow-bound wilderness receded as the chopper climbed. It would take longer for the memories to fade. Joe was determined they wouldn't become his nightmares in the way of 9-11. And he was equally determined to do everything in his power to keep his family together—and safe.

11:00 p.m.

Kate lay in her own bed, sleeping on her back with one arm flung above her head and the other wrapped around Jefferson.

Maggie's amazing dog had lifted his head the moment she'd appeared in the doorway. She and Jefferson stared at each other now, communicating without words.

We found her. She's safe. We won't lose her again. Not ever.

Joe came up behind her and peered over her shoulder. "She okay?" he whispered.

"Yes." Maggie half turned to smile at him. "For the fifteenth time tonight."

"Go ahead. Call me a helicopter dad. I don't mind."

Kate stirred and they watched from the doorway to make sure she wouldn't start tossing with nightmares. There was nothing anxious in her movements, nothing to alarm. She was just an ordinary healthy teenager, sleeping deeply after her extraordinary feats.

Maggie put her finger to her lips and led the way back

into the den. Joe had kept the fire going and turned on the Christmas tree lights. He'd even made hot chocolate with a dash of cinnamon. Served in Christmas mugs. The scent intoxicated. It was Maggie's favorite holiday indulgence. Forget the sugar and calories.

She sank onto the sofa and he sat down beside her. Close. A good sign. Usually he sat in the recliner across the room.

"I thought we deserved a treat," he said.

"You bet." She lifted her cup, thought briefly of proposing a toast, but quickly rejected the idea. What on earth would it be? *Cheers* seemed trite after the last two days. And how could you possibly reduce what had happened to them into a sound bite?

"Mags, I talked to Roger."

"When?" Since their return from the nightmare, she'd tried to be aware of every little thing happening in her house. Constant vigilance was exhausting.

"While you were in the shower." Joe set his Christmas mug on the coffee table. Rudolph with his red nose and a goofy grin on his face. The mug looked so ordinary, so homey and hopeful, Maggie had to battle back tears. She desperately wanted ordinary. "He said the body in the barrel at the West-berg house belonged to Harvey Westberg, Jonathan's father. He wanted us to know ahead of the news."

"You're kidding. Did the monster kill his own dad?"

"No. Jonathan thought his dad had left them when he was four years. When he heard the news, he started singing like a bird. He said his mom was an expert with weapons and kept a Winchester rifle and a Colt .45 in her bedroom. Chances are she put the bullet hole in Harvey's skull."

"What about the girls that little creep killed? And what he did to Kate? Is some high-powered defense attorney going to come forward and help him wiggle out of that?"

"He confessed to killing both girls and kidnapping Kate.

And Katie will be a powerful witness for the prosecution. We don't have to worry about him getting off and coming after her again."

Maggie set her coffee cup on the table and leaned back against the sofa.

"You should go to bed," Joe said. "I'll put Kate's things under the tree."

"Are you kidding? You think I'd miss playing Santa because of that evil troll?"

"That's my girl."

Joe grinned at her, and Maggie didn't feel the least bit silly that the two of them still put Santa gifts under the tree for a nineteen year old. Kate had figured out Santa fourteen years ago, but all three of them loved the tradition. It was part of the magic of Christmas.

They scurried around, digging gifts out of hiding places and wrapping them together, Joe making sharp corners on the holiday wrapping paper and Maggie tying the bows. When they'd finished, Joe said all they needed was a plate of cookies and a glass of milk waiting by the fireside for the jolly old man in red.

"No," she said. "It needs one more gift."

"I thought this was it."

"Not quite."

Maggie hurried to their bedroom and removed the gift from her lingerie drawer. She couldn't wait till morning. She wouldn't sleep a wink that night wondering if her big secret would be a hit or a miss.

Sure, she and Joe had talked about the twins last night. But when your life and the life of everyone you loved was on the line, it was easier to unburden your soul. It was more natural, somehow, to believe that airing long-held grievances would make them vanish.

Maggie knew it wouldn't be that simple to repair years of

damage. But she had to start somewhere. And she preferred to start in private. Just the two of them.

Uncertainty nagged at her as she went back to the den, holding the gift behind her back. Joe looked up and smiled.

"There you are!"

"Here I am." She held out the slender package, wrapped in gold foil and tied with a gold bow. "I have a gift."

"For me?"

"No. For us." When she handed it over, he lifted an eyebrow. Such a sexy, sardonic look. She hadn't seen it in a long time.

"You want me to open it now?"

"Please."

He took his time untying the bow and setting it aside, slicing the tape with his pocketknife and unfolding the paper so she could recycle it for next year. Joe was like that. Methodical.

No. That sounded boring, something her husband had never been.

He was careful.

When he pulled the gift from its wrappings and stood there, speechless, her tension went up a notch.

"Aren't you going to say anything, Joe?"

"When did you get these?"

"A few weeks ago." Her heart squeezed. What was going through his mind?

"You knew what you wanted, even then?"

"Yes. If you'll remember, only day before yesterday I made a fool of myself over you in the kitchen."

"You never make a fool of yourself, Maggie. Why didn't you tell me last night when we talked?"

"I didn't want a fresh start to be intertwined with the most horrible thing that has ever happened to us."

His grin was a sudden and blooming thing, the spring-thaw moment she'd waited years to see.

"Hawaii in January." He glanced at the tickets, still smiling. "Just us."

"Paradise for two."

"How are we going to pull this off?"

He'd said *we*. The two of them. Together.

"Kate will be back in school. Roger and Clair said they'd be surrogate parents for her and Jefferson, both. And Kate will be glad to spend some extra time with Teresa."

"Hmmm." Joe looked deep in thought, and Maggie had a moment's doubt.

She'd bought the tickets long before a raving madman had kidnapped her daughter. When the time came, could she fly off to a sunny climate and leave her daughter behind? Could her husband?

"You're not worried about leaving her are you, Joe?"

"Are you kidding me? After what she did, maybe we ought to take her along as a bodyguard."

Joe reached for her, and their laughter brought Kate and Jefferson both to the door. Their dog wagged his tail and their daughter studied them with sleepy confusion. Suddenly, comprehension dawned.

"Am I interrupting anything? I hope."

"Yes." Maggie and Joe spoke in unison, then Joe said, "Go back to bed, sleepyhead."

"Not a chance! Merry Christmas, you two." Grinning Kate marched into the den and wrapped her arms around both parents.

Yes, Maggie thought. *This*.

It was the perfect moment. Love spun with a silver thread so strong the Carter family could withstand anything thrown at them by nature and man. Gratitude so deep it was endless.

And hope that even a monster storm and a monster killer couldn't stamp out.*

THANKS FOR READING! **If you enjoyed this book, please do leave a review.**

Read on for a sneak peek of the next STORM WATCH novel, *Snow Blind* by Cindy Gerard.

SNEAK PEEK

SNOW BLIND
STORMWATCH, Book 6
by Cindy Gerard

Prologue

Rome, Italy
June, 18 months ago

Josh Haskins maneuvered her royal high-brow, Princess Anastasia Gerhardt – aka: Ms. Blond, beautiful and bratty – firmly behind him and away from the pack of bar lizards, fending them off as he backed toward the alley exit of the mobbed party bar.

True to form, the princess had dragged him into the middle of the obscenely rich and spoiled Italian jet set scene, dressed like a designer slut in her lipstick red mini dress and attracting every stray dog and lone wolf with a yen to howl.

"This is so bogus," he muttered beneath a grinding rock beat and a full on testosterone blast. They came at her like worker drones flocking to the queen bee. No one, however, was allowed to taste her honey. Not on his watch.

Good Lord. *This* was his first official, full-fledged assignment as a Rapid Response Alliance operative? Was he hunting terrorists in the middle of the Congo? Running recon on a snatch and grab op in the Middle East? Even guarding a diplomatic cadre to a top secret security meeting? Oh, hell, no.

His first *mission* was to: A) keep the princess happy, B) keep the princess safe, and C) keep the princess from creating an international incident.

At the moment, C was giving him the most trouble. That and his simmering temper.

"You don't want to do this," Josh warned as an inebriated Romeo, stunning in a black, silk shirt opened to his navel, a boatload of bling hanging around his neck, and skin-tight do-you-like-my-package leather pants, separated himself from the pack and made a move toward the princess.

The wannabe paramour took one look at the dark rage on Josh's face and thought better of his decision. Not so drunk after all, Josh was happy to report. The problem was, at least ten other contenders were circling the campfire, ready to take a crack at roasting Anastasia's marshmallows.

"It wasn't enough that you had to incite a riot in that almost dress," he sputtered to her royal pain-in-the ass. "You had to hop up on the bar. Had to pour champagne down your cleavage and invite every Tom, Dick, and Horny to come and lick it off."

Behind him, Anastasia giggled. "A girl's gotta have fun."

Josh glanced over his shoulder and glared into flirty, fiery, blue eyes. Blue like a summer sky he'd thought the first time he'd seen them. Ha. Blue like the color his balls were gonna be if he didn't get her out of this den of dickwads and soon.

He ducked a flying beer bottle, shoved the princess more securely behind him, and swore to God that if he got her out of this mess without creating that international incident she was bent on making, he was going to throw her over his knee and whale the tar out of her sexy little behind. PC or not.

"So help me God, Ant*ipasto*," he grumbled as he held back the pack crocked on vino and hell bent on tasting the Princess's bountiful cleavage, "when I get you back to the hotel, we're going to have us a little come to Jesus meeting."

"Sounds positively ... spiritual," the princess of the newly sovereign nation of Slarovia purred into his ear in perfect English as she dug red lacquered nails that matched her dress deeper into his shoulders.

She squealed then ducked behind him when a particularly brave – read: stupid – admirer made a grab at her. A quick chop to his arm and a well-placed knee to his breadbasket dispensed with Stupid.

Another one bites the dust.

The floor was already littered with the guys' 'brothers in rut' who'd thought they were going to worship at the altar of the ultimate one night stand.

Another bottle flew by just as Josh made it to the exit and backed the princess through the door and into a heat drenched Italian night pungent with the scents of garlic and wine and trouble.

Man, this sucked. Josh Haskins had never quit on anything in his life, yet five bullet-sweating, tongue-biting days into this assignment watch dogging the high-maintenance, party animal, Anastasia, and saving her blue-blooded hide from one scrape after another, and he was ready to cash in his chips.

"Babysitter. That's all I am. A glorified babysitter," he grumbled as he dragged her away from the bar at a brisk clip and finally left the wannabe bad boys behind.

Pale street lights and a rumbling rock beat leaked out of the bar, following them as he hustled her down the narrow, cobblestone strada.

"Slow down, would you? I can't run in these heels."

He ignored her sputtering protests and tried to remember why he'd agreed to this assignment. Oh, yeah. Something about saving the world.

Well, hell, what red-blooded American patriot could resist a stab at doing just that? He'd been born for the job. Or so complained any woman who had ever gotten too close and thought she might have a chance of taking over as the number one priority in his life.

So, no. Josh hadn't been able to resist. When he'd finally received the invitation to join RRA and had been offered this cock-eyed assignment, he'd have said yes to latrine duty.

"Yes, sir, I'm up for anything, sir." Even though it meant that Josh's rookie run as a new recruit for the elite and clandestine international organization involved playing bodyguard to a spoiled brat of a newly minted European princess.

"I said, slow down!" The princess demanded, putting on the skids.

Satisfied that they were well clear of the nightclub, Josh stopped, turned and glared at five feet six inches of cover girl curves and cascading blond hair. Who could blame those poor Casanovas? This woman put the sex in sex appeal. She also put the Tick in ticked off – which he was. Royally.

"You know," Josh said, nailing her with a look, "if you had the sense God gave a goat, I wouldn't have to drag you out of one scrape after another."

"Not up to the assignment, Haskins?"

Baiting him? She was actually *baiting* him? After all the crap he'd put up with in the last five days?

"Fine. Have your fun," he ground out as the knot at the end of his rope finally unraveled. "Only from now you can have it without me. I've had it with this gig."

And he'd had it with the woman, who, despite her princess to peasant regard for him, somehow managed to rile both his anger and his testosterone levels to new heights. Did. Not. Compute.

"Come on." He latched on to her wrist and stormed off again, as angry at her as he was at himself for letting her sex-goddess looks get to him. "I'm taking you back to the hotel. Then we're going to see about getting you a new babysitter. I'm officially turning in my nanny badge."

Hell. He'd thought that once he'd made the grade, cracked the RRA requirements and become an operative that he'd be knee deep in international espionage.

So much for what he'd thought.

Slowly, Josh became aware that she was laughing.

Laughing.

He stopped – and she ran smack into him. He latched on to both arms to steady her then set her none too gently away. "So happy to entertain you."

"Oh, you do." Her grin widened. "I wondered how hard I was going to have to push you before you finally snapped."

He glared at the top of her head. She'd started tugging off her sky high stilettos.

"Sweet heaven, that feels good." Standing bare-foot on the cobblestones, she tossed both shoes over her shoulder into a hedge, giving them a good ride.

He looked from the flying heels back to her face. "*How hard you were going to have to push to finally make me snap?*"

"Oh, for Pete's sake, Haskins. Lighten up. You passed,

okay? And none too soon for my taste. I was running out of stunts."

He waited three beats, watching her eyes as she dragged a tumble of hair away from her face. "What the hell are you talking about?"

"Okay," she said conversationally, like he wasn't glaring daggers and contemplating wrapping his hands around that lovely slim neck and wringing it until her tongue turned as blue as her eyes.

"Here's the deal, Haskins. I was a test."

Another three beat pause while he watched her with ever narrowing eyes. "A test."

"Well, *Anastasia* was a test. For me too, if it's any consolation. In fact, there is no such animal – or in this case no such *party* animal."

She smiled.

He didn't.

"Lieutenant Cara Graves, European base, RRA Headquarters, Barcelona. And you were my cross to bear as much as Anastasia was yours."

He felt his temperature rise right along with his hackles. "Cross to bear?"

She sighed. "As you may have surmised by now, I'm not a princess. My name is not Anastasia Gehart-"

"Got that part," he said through his clenched jaw.

"I'm an RRA operative who was given the assignment of testing your mettle ten ways from Sunday to make certain you were up for any task – even one as seemingly trivial and demeaning as babysitting a brat.

"So cool your jets, Haskins," she added, not even a tiny bit rattled when he continued to glare bullets at her. "Just settle down and congratulate yourself on a job well done."

She extended her hand. "You've passed muster. Welcome aboard."

Duped. He'd been duped like a UN weapons inspector.

He ignored her hand. "This was all a set up?"

She shrugged. "Call it an initiation. Someday, I might tell you what they did to initiate me." She smiled again and tried for another handshake.

"I don't give a damn what they did to you." He spun around and headed for the hotel. "You and RRA can take your muster and your initiation and stick it where the sun don't shine."

"Hmmm. Never said you were a poor sport on your application."

He flipped her the bird and kept walking.

"You *really* want to miss your first *real* field assignment?" she called after him.

Josh stopped, turned, glared at her where she stood in a pool of light cast from a street lantern. Golden hair a gorgeous, messy tangle. Blue eyes challenging and amused. The thin strap of her short, slinky red dress, sliding off her left shoulder.

For an instant, he had to remind himself how ticked off he was. "Oh. A *real* assignment?" he spat sarcastically. "What? The queen of England due for a party run and needs a driver?"

The husky sound of her laugh had something other than his anger rising again.

"Oh, it's waaay better than that."

He considered her with enough skepticism to fill the Coliseum. "It had better be."

She'd walked closer and in a low and deadly serious voice told him.

Good. God. It was good all right. As good as it got.

Twelve hours later
   Barcelona, Spain

Josh waited patiently in the dimly lit situation room; adrenaline mainlined directly into his blood stream; his tension peaked right along with his curiosity. His ALICE pack sat on the floor beside his M4 assault rifle. He was pumped and ready for this mission. His first real mission with RRA.

And he was ready to meet his new CO. A fellow warrior – not a smart mouthed wasp of an agent who played the role of diva far too well.

Initiation my ass. Damn, he was glad to be free of Anastasia ... make that Cara, he corrected with a grunt. He'd had enough of both of them, thank you very much.

He checked his watch. Less than a quarter of an hour until they deployed. The assignment was plum, as she'd promised: Infiltrate an outer island off the Malaysian coast and the hideout of the terrorist cell, Death Toll. Find the plant that produced lethal nerve gas then neutralize and destroy both the facility and the stockpile of the deadly poison. Added bonus: Capture or eliminate the terrorists responsible.

Piece of cake, he thought with a grim look at the terrain map tacked to the wall and hoped his lawyer had finished the last minute changes to his will. If anything happened to him, he wanted his nephew taken care of.

A door opened behind him. Josh snapped to attention without turning around. Only one other person had clearance for this room at this hour. His new CO.

"At ease, Sergeant."

Josh stopped breathing. Was pretty sure his heart stopped beating, too.

He knew that voice. What he didn't know, was why he was hearing it now.

"I said at ease."

He turned slowly as Lieutenant Cara Graves walked into the room, combat ready in jungle camos, M16 in hand, a modified ALICE pack strapped to her back.

"What the hell are you doing here?" Josh finally managed when he could get his mouth to work.

"Wanna rephrase that, Sergeant?"

Josh swallowed, eyes dead ahead as Lt. Graves moved to stand directly in front of him.

"What the hell are you doing here, *sir?*" he repeated crisply.

But deep in his gut, he already knew. Damn it all to hell, he knew.

"You got a problem working with a female operative, Haskins?"

He had a problem working with *this* female operative.

"No, sir," he gritted out, knowing that if he voiced his objections he'd be off the op faster than you could say, *You blew it, buddy*.

"Got a problem with a female outranking you?"

Lord, help him.

"No, sir."

"Good answer."

Oh, she knew he was ticked.

"Good." She headed for the door. "Then grab your gear. Transport bird's waiting to take us to the Philippines. And pull the bug out of your butt, sergeant. Let's go save the world."

December 22
1:20 pm

"Remember that you heard it here first folks."

Don McDowell flashed pearly white teeth to the camera and stacked his pages of copy on the desk in front of him. "KCRG TV 9 first alert weather is not afraid to predict that the Cedar Rapids viewing area is either going to dodge a major bullet or we're going to get hit with potentially the most massive winter blizzard seen in this area in almost a century."

Julie Paul, the evening anchor, gave Don a comical smile. "Wow, Don. Could you *be* any more ambiguous?"

Don chuckled and the camera followed the weatherman as he rose from his desk and moved in front of an Iowa weather map swirling with radar simulations, snowflakes and as an added humorous touch, question marks.

"I couldn't be more vague if I tried, Julie. Let me try to explain why the forecast is such a mystery."

Don manipulated the map with the touch of his finger to include several western and northern states as well as the southern part of Canada. "Many of you have been aware of Blizzard Holly, whose genesis was in Canada before she swooped down into Montana, Colorado, back up to Nebraska, then east into South Dakota."

He turned back to face the camera. "Holly is currently

blasting Minnesota and all indications are that she has no predilection to blow herself out anytime soon. Based on the route she's taken she may – or may not," he added with a smile of caution, "find her way down through east central Iowa.

"Why, you might ask, can't I be more specific? Well, there are so many variables in play as of now that even the National Weather Service's state of the art computers can't pinpoint the storm's path or its full effect on Iowa. Forecast details will become clearer and more accurate as this blizzard keeps churning through Minnesota.

"Those variables include a low pressure system here." He used a hand-held remote to zero in on the map. "The jet stream over here, upper level winds, and how much cold air is in place when, or if, the storm arrives. Even a relatively small change in this low pressure system, for instance, can make a huge difference. A shift one way can create blizzard conditions while the other way could bring only a light dusting of snow."

His expression became serious. "Here at TV 9, we realize how critical it is for you all to know what weather you may be facing in the near future. It's almost Christmas, after all. Many of you have travel plans or family planning to visit you. For that reason, we're taking a very cautious approach to predicting the effect Holly will have on our viewing area."

The camera moved in for a close up. "Rest assured, we are monitoring this storm like NASA monitors a rocket launch. We'll cut into regular programming if necessary to keep you up to date on Holly's path and velocity and the severity of the snowfall, the wind and the cold.

"In the meantime, look for cloudy skies tomorrow with a high of twenty-three degrees Fahrenheit and north winds no more than five miles per hour. Sunrise will be at 7:31am and we should have a beautiful sunset at 4:38pm.

"Have a great rest of your evening and all day tomorrow. Julie – back to you..."

CHAPTER 1

December 23rd

T'was the season. Family. Friends. Food. Ho. Ho. Ho. The team was definitely due for some R & R. They weren't going to get it. Not yet. At least Cara wasn't. Neither, she'd decided, was Haskins.

Another flight announcement over the din of the crowds waiting at Chicago, O'Hare, Terminal C, had her rising wearily to her feet.

"That's us." Cara shouldered her carry-on and got in line with the passengers boarding the December 23rd, 12:10 pm flight from Chicago, to Cedar Rapids, Iowa.

Her Christmas holiday. Not how Cara had seen it playing out. The RRA jet had delivered them from NYC to Chicago an hour ago but it was commercial from here on in. They didn't want to draw any undue attention. A private Gulfstream flying into the small airport in Cedar Rapids this close to Christmas probably wouldn't raise any red flags but it could draw some speculative attention and that was the last thing they wanted.

Keeping a low profile was already a bit tricky considering that Haskins drew the interest of most women and a few envious men. It was human nature. When you saw a six foot four, ruggedly attractive, mature male who could easily pose for the cover of MEN's HEALTH magazine, it was hard not to stare. Especially when his gaze landed, even briefly, on you.

Steel gray. Piercing. Aged to perfection from creases fed by the sun and combat and living on the edge.

So low profile? Not so much. Not with Haskins on the scene. Still, it was economy seats and a valiant attempt at playing average Jane and Joe. Carry on only. There hadn't been time for packing so they'd each brought only specific technical surveillance gadgetry that they'd need and couldn't buy when they got there. RRA had provided them both with night vision glasses equipped with infrared thermal imaging cameras. As far as she knew, they were the first to field test this new version.

Otherwise, if they needed anything else they'd have to buy it locally. And hope everything wasn't sold out this close to Christmas. Guess they'd soon find out.

Icy air stung Cara's cheeks, making her eyes water as they crossed the open tarmac toward the small airbus that would deliver them to Cedar Rapids in under an hour.

Haskins, a North Carolina boy, tucked his chin into the collar of his jacket but didn't grumble about the cold. Haskins never grumbled. He glared. He simmered. Sometimes, he even boiled. But like a good soldier, he followed orders and did his job. Did it with precision and skill and if he had a problem with her performance as the team leader and as his CO, he hadn't shown it on a single one of their many missions during the last year and a half.

He clearly, however, had a problem with her. With being around her. With sometimes being very near to her in the often close confines required by their operations.

She wasn't mistaken about that. She felt something. The crackle. The sizzle. Even the occasional fissure in his concentration. And none of it had anything to do with his test as Anastasia's baby sitter. No. This had nothing to do with Anastasia and everything to do with Cara Graves.

Aware of him walking with purpose across the tarmac

behind her, she kept her eyes dead ahead, shivering against the brutal cold as she climbed the open jet stairs. In her experience, there weren't many places colder than a flat, windy tarmac in the middle of winter.

She quickly found her seat in the sixty-passenger air bus and dropped heavily into it. Low on sleep from the scramble to make this mission, she was determined to at least catch a power nap on the hour long flight.

The flight to Iowa. A flyover state. Corn, if she remembered right. Cows. Oh, yeah. And a state fair made famous in the vintage movie Music Man and for a cow made of butter. Homeland, USA. Not exactly a hotbed of terrorist activity. Cold as a freezer the end of December – just like it was in Chicago, NYC, and Boston.

She had high hopes that with any luck, this would be a quick recon mission. They'd be in and out. Twenty-four hours max. Then she'd head back to Boston in time for Christmas dinner at her sister's. She had big plans to gorge herself on pumpkin pie, zone out to the crackling of an apple wood fire, and watch her gorgeous five year old twin nieces plow into the presents she'd brought them.

Sometimes she wanted that. Home, hearth, kids and a dog. Yeah, especially around the holidays, she questioned her dangerous and solitary career choice. But then a mission would come up. The adrenaline would start rushing through her bloodstream and she knew why she did what she did.

Someday. Maybe. While she was still young enough to have children and not too old to learn how to cook.

Smiling at herself for lapsing into a bit of melancholy, she stowed her gear under the seat, buckled herself in and closed her eyes, peripherally aware of Haskins buckling in across the aisle.

His broad shoulders and long legs over-filled the skimpy seat. She didn't have to look at him to know that his steely gray eyes betrayed no emotion. As usual. The man was a bit of an enigma. And she found him a bit too interesting. That was all going to change.

Right now, she needed that power nap. If she was lucky, she'd be asleep before the landing gear tucked into the belly of the jet. But instead of sleeping, she found herself thinking about Haskins again.

Why had she chosen him for this mini mission? Well, not exactly chosen. He'd volunteered like a good team member so the others could enjoy their holiday with family. Which worked out fine because if he hadn't stepped up, she'd been going to tap him for the op anyway.

She'd decided it was time to admit that she had a little problem with him. A problem a commanding officer didn't need with a subordinate. A problem that was universally wrong under any operational circumstances.

This was her chance to confront and dissuade said problem before anything out of order happened between them. To face and conquer it without interference from the team. That's why she'd wanted just the two of them on this low risk, low adrenaline recon. Cooler minds do prevail. She needed to clear the air because if she didn't, she was afraid she knew where this was heading. Sex. Maybe even something more.

Sex and work didn't mix. Especially with their kind of work. Life and death situations didn't allow for even minor slip ups that a distracting physical relationship could possibly initiate.

You didn't think with your head when you were involved with someone whose life was on the line. Made stupid decisions based on emotions instead of logic. Took stupid chances.

So, yes. It was time to sort it out with him. Admit that the attraction wasn't just on his end. Agree that they needed to face it, forget it, and forge on without acting on their more primal urges which, without a doubt, could jeopardize their future missions.

So she'd fix it. Nip it in the bud.

Satisfied that her secondary mission to clear the air with Haskins was a go, she fell asleep.

Yet as she slept, she dreamed. Unfortunately, Haskins was in the dream. Again.

Naked.

Again.

***

The Eastern Iowa airport was small but modern and efficient. As soon as they disembarked the plane, they rode down the single escalator and headed straight toward the rental car counters.

"Better get a 4-wheel drive," Cara said, otherwise deferring the rest of the details to Haskins to select their ride.

Outside the terminal windows, a light mix of freezing rain and snow had started falling. She didn't like the looks of that but since she couldn't do anything about it, she turned to her GPS to acquaint herself with the Cedar Rapids area.

Five minutes later, Haskins met her by the exit door pocketing a set of keys.

"Everyone had the same idea," he said.

She looked up as he held out the paperwork for the rental.

"Best I could do is a small SUV. Let's hope it's got good traction. And did we know we were running into snow?"

She let out air between puffed cheeks. "Weather reports have been sketchy. Last I heard, the snow was going to veer back north but, apparently, we're getting a little Christmas surprise. Let's regroup on the road and hope we're in and out before the worst of the weather sets in."

After cleaning the dusting of snow off their white SUV, they stowed their bags in the back seat and Haskins settled in behind the wheel.

"Head north toward I-380. We've got a little ways to go."

"Read me in," he said, as they cleared the airport parking complex.

Need to know was standard mission protocol and up until this moment, Haskins hadn't had a clue what they were about.

"Palo, Iowa, about twenty minutes north of here, is the site of an aging nuclear energy plant."

"Still in use?" He flipped the turn signal and pulled out onto the on ramp.

"As of now, yes. It's due to close in the next year or so, though. This plant has been in commission since the 70's so obviously it's got some years on it. In any event," she continued then caught a gasp when the SUV hit an icy patch and fishtailed sideways.

"Sorry." Haskins let off the gas, regained control and they continued on their way.

Windshield wipers worked at slapping away the snow that had picked up a little in intensity. The defrost fan ran overtime to keep the glass fog free.

"In any event," Cara began again, relieved to see that Haskins had regained a solid handle on the vehicle, "RRA received a report from NSA. They intercepted a burst of cyber-chatter from an IP address in Cedar Rapids. This was a week ago."

"And this nuc plant was mentioned," he concluded.

"Actually, no." She smiled grimly. "The plant was never mentioned, but Armageddon was - several times. Along with some veiled phrases that are typical of extremist groups wanting to make a big noise about a big bang.

"Before NSA could zero in on absolutes, though, whoever was communicating using this IP address got wise and started encrypting all of their messages. Then, two days ago, they went totally silent."

"Which raised some red flags," Haskins deduced. "Still a stretch to think we're going to find Armageddon in the making. From locals. In Iowa."

"Apparently this same IP user had been on their radar a couple of years ago for much of the same kind of chatter but went silent then, too."

"Until last week when they picked up this new communication. Still," he said, sounding dubious. "Like I said. It's a stretch."

"True. But stranger things have happened," she reminded him.

"Yeah. 9-11," Haskins mulled grimly. "Seems I remember a connection to one of the hijackers and Cedar Rapids."

"There was that," she agreed quietly and felt the overwhelming rush of anger and anguish and patriotism that had been the impetus for her Army enlistment and ultimately her service in the RRA.

She'd been a kid when the Towers fell, but she'd never forget the images on TV and the utter despair she'd felt for the victims and the country. Her future had been decided then and there. She wanted to serve. She *needed* to serve and her focus from that moment on was doing just that. As soon as she turned turned eighteen, she joined the Army, worked her way up to a noncom officer, furthered her education and advanced through both the service and her degrees to her position at RRA.

She'd led missions all over the world. Asia. Soviet Union. Iraq, Syria, Afghanistan, Central America. There wasn't a

Third World or sophisticated European country where she hadn't laid down footprints.

Now? Now she was Iowa. The thought that she was within driving distance to the Field of Dreams as opposed to the killing fields of Cambodia made her smile. She was due for a cush assignment. She was banking on this sneak and peep being it.

Beside her, Haskins drove in thoughtful silence. She took the time to pull up the RRA message on her phone and reread the directive in case she'd missed anything. The orders had been short on info and long on speculation. Because of that sudden flurry of cyber-chatter over a very recent and very brief window of time, NSA alerted RRA to scramble together a team and check things out immediately.

Everything had moved at warp speed after that. They'd been wheels up out of LaGuardia within two hours of their return from their most recent mission in Somalia. Just the two of them. Traveling light and lean while Christmas travelers hummed along with the holiday music piped over the airport PA system between called and canceled flights.

She closed the message and stared out at the interstate which had become a ribbon of white. "Let's hope it's a wild goose chase."

"Your Christmas wish?"

She smiled. "Close enough."

They both knew that at any given time, there were details similar to theirs checking out threats, sometimes finding nothing, sometimes squashing a real menace that the general public would never hear anything about.

"The life of a shadow warrior," Haskins said with a self-effacing smile. "Missed holidays, missed opportunities. Nothing but selflessness and sacrifice."

"Yeah, that," Cara said, appreciating this little glimpse of his sense of humor – something she'd rarely seen. "Regardless, whoever these people are, we need to find out if they're some wannabe bad guys just talking to hear themselves talk or if they're the real deal and they're actually planning something."

"How did NSA settle on this nuc plant as the likely target?"

"Process of elimination. There are other potential targets in the area, yes, but none as target rich and as capable of producing death and destruction as this."

"Got it. So has security at the nuc plant been notified?"

"Not yet. No need getting everyone's tail in a twist if it turns out to be a false alarm."

He nodded. "So we're strictly recon and assessment."

"That's the directive, yes. We need to get a read on: a) if we're truly looking at a terrorist cell, b) and if so, if they're actually planning something - which would most likely be destruction or damage to the plant, c) if they have a plan, how far developed it is, and d) if they have the means to pull it off."

He grunted, tapped his thumbs on the wheel. "And it had to be at Christmas. Of course."

"If we're looking at jihadists, then yes. It's the most celebrated Christian holiday. But, if they're home grown and zealot, say environmentalists who are opposed to nuclear power on principal, they might simply want to take advantage of the winter weather to sneak in."

"If they're *environmentalists*," Haskins pointed out, "then they're not looking to do any real damage."

"Right. These far out groups are happy to stage mock attacks just to point out the vulnerabilities of nuclear power, hoping to get nuc plants shut down all over the world."

"The fools don't think about the havoc they create. Or that they could actually get killed themselves in their staged drama." Haskins stared straight ahead, his jaw tight. "Or that if they're successful, a bevy of copycat attacks could be staged all over the world.

"The problem is, one of those attacks could be real then everyone's caught off guard as radioactive waste is released and we start seeing the consequences down the road."

Cara heard him loud and clear. "Still, I vote for environmentalists as the best case scenario. They don't generally deal in bombs and rocket propelled grenades."

"True that. But, let's say it is jihadists," Haskins hypothesized. "Al-Qaeda. ISIS. And they want to blow the plant. If they want to do the most damage we're not exactly looking at a highly populated area. There are other nuc plants near much more densely populated cities."

"Actually, they *could* do a lot of damage here. Think of Palo as the hub in a wheel connecting Chicago, Twin Cities, Omaha, St. Louis, and Kansas City and you've got plenty of population. The Mississippi is also a stone's throw from the plant. There would be major devastation all the way down to the Gulf if the river is contaminated with nuclear waste."

"Guess I need to brush up on my geography. Hadn't realized where we are now in relation to Chicago, et al." He slowed down for a semi when it joined traffic from an on ramp. "How much farther to Palo?"

"Not far. But this cell – and we'll call it a cell for expediency sake from now on - is not based in Palo. Per Intel, the IP address is from a computer in an apartment on the north side of Cedar Rapids."

"Why not in Palo?" Haskins glanced sideways at her.

"Because Palo is a barely a town. It tops out at around a thousand people. There'd be no place to hide there without sticking out like an elephant in a strawberry patch.

"So, no. Cedar Rapids is about nine miles from the plant and close enough for a base of operation. Again, if there is an operation. And we're going to proceed as though there is."

"Do we have a head count? Any ID? Pictures? Names? Faces of these suspected cell members?"

She shook her head. "I wish."

"So we've got nothing, is what you're saying?"

"Pretty much."

"And yet they're thinking home grown – whether we're talking Jihad or environmental terror?"

She shrugged. "Only because there've been no links or threads to any known groups from the Middle East or parts unknown to this area. Facial recognition software at major airports would have spotted any ringers entering the country and headed this way and they've tagged nothing."

He pushed out a grunt. "You're forgetting that we've got a porous southern and northern border that pretty much ensures terrorists could enter with a ridiculous amount of ease."

"True, but the chatter has been pinpointed coming only from this apartment with only local contacts, which indicates they're confined to Cedar Rapids.

"While we're here," Cara continued, "both NSA and RRA are all over social media trying to find and connect more dots. We'll hear from them with details if they find a suspect. And any partial Intel we gather – names, photos – we can feed to them and they'll run it through the systems, see what they find."

"Could be a long established sleeper cell as well," he said after giving it more thought. "Planted by some offshoot of Al-Queda or ISIS just waiting for the right place, right time to pull the trigger."

Before she could comment, a weather warning buzzed in on Cara's phone.

"Perfect," she said after opening up the bulletin then reading it out loud for Haskins' benefit.

"A southern boy like you is going to love this. National

Weather Service just issued a blizzard watch. A huge storm could approach central through northeast Iowa within the next twenty-four hours. Heavy snowfall with accumulations of twelve to twenty-four inches of blowing and drifting snow and subzero windchill factors. Underlying ice will make road travel difficult to impossible."

"Sounds positively chilling."

She glanced across the front seat at him. "I guess a watch is better than a warning. Let's hope the weatherman's wrong or that we can stay ahead of this storm. Otherwise, it looks like we might be up for mission impossible."

Haskins braked lightly as a vehicle ahead of them skidded sideways on a patch of ice before the driver regained control.*

THE STORMWATCH SERIES

Holly, the worst winter storm in eighty years...

Holly blows in with subzero temperatures, ice and snow better measured in feet than in inches, and leaves devastation and destruction in its wake. But, in a storm, the weather isn't the only threat—and those are the stories told in the STORMWATCH series. Track the storm through these six chilling romantic suspense novels:

FROZEN GROUND by Debra Webb, Montana
DEEP FREEZE by Vicki Hinze, Colorado
WIND CHILL by Rita Herron, Nebraska
BLACK ICE by Regan Black, South Dakota
SNOW BRIDES by Peggy Webb, Minnesota
SNOW BLIND by Cindy Gerard, Iowa

Get the Books at Amazon

ABOUT THE AUTHOR

Peggy Webb is the award-winning, *USA Today* bestselling author of almost 100 novels. The former instructor of writing at Mississippi Sate University writes in multiple genres under her own name and two pen names, **Elaine Hussey** and **Anna Michaels.** Reviewers dubbed Peggy "comedic genius" for her *Southern Cousins Mystery* series and "one of the Southern literary greats" for her acclaimed literary fiction. A native Mississippian, Peggy lives in a writer's cottage tucked among flower gardens where she has quietly become the most prolific writer her state has ever produced.

Peggy also writes screenplays and has penned more than 200 magazine humor columns. Several of her books, including the *Southern Cousins Mysteries,* have been optioned for film. She holds a B.A. from Mississippi University for Women and an M.A. from the University of Mississippi. A gifted musician and actress, Peggy loves taking the stage at Tupelo Community Theater, singing in a 60-voice church choir and playing her vintage baby grand. She particularly loves blues and has stacks of blues lyrics she composed for her own amusement, including *Why Ain't You Dead Yet.* Peggy loves hearing from readers. Follow her on her two blogs at her websites www.peggywebb.com and www.elainehussey.com as well as on Facebook, Twitter. Goodreads, BookBub and her Amazon Author Page. Sign up for Peggy's newsletter at www.peggywebb.com.

ALSO BY PEGGY WEBB

(A sampling of Peggy's books, selected by the author)

Stars to Lead Me Home

The Sweetest Hallelujah
(written as Elaine Hussey)

Magnolia Wild Vanishes
(A Charmed Cat Mystery, Book 1)

Elvis and the Devil in Disguise
(A Southern Cousins Mystery, Book 13

Elvis and the Blue Suede Bones
(A Southern Cousins Mystery, Book 12)

Elvis and the Pink Cadillac Corpse
(A Southern Cousins Mystery, Book 11)

Get a printable list of all Peggy's books at :
www.peggywebb.com

DON'T MISS

THE EXPLOSIVE SUSPENSE SERIES

A ground-breaking, fast paced 4-book suspense series that will keep you turning pages until the end. Reviews describe BREAKDOWN as "unique," "brilliant" and "the best series of the year." The complete series includes **the dead girl** by Debra Webb, **so many secrets** by Vicki Hinze, **all the lies** by Peggy Webb and **what she knew** by Regan Black. You'll want all four books of the thrilling BREAKDOWN series!